"I'm not as easy to read as you think I am, cowboy," Gabi said.

Jess paused to look down at her. She blinked innocently and her smile widened. He had known her all of thirty minutes and he'd already figured her out. "I never said you were easy to read. Matter of fact, I have a feeling you probably work real hard at being complicated."

Gabi chuckled behind him. "You know what?"

He was walking past her with the other calf and paused to let it loose before facing her. "What?" he asked, grinning because there was nothing else to do.

"I like you even if you are bossy. I'm going to have fun keeping you on your toes."

If he'd had a hat, he'd have tipped it at her, but it was somewhere downstream stuck in the mud. Instead he just nodded. "Have at it. I like a woman who keeps me guessing."

"Then you're going to love me," she quipped.

Books by Debra Clopton

Love Inspired

*The Trouble with Lacy Brown
*And Baby Makes Five
*No Place Like Home
*Dream a Little Dream
*Meeting Her Match
*Operation: Married by Christmas
*Next Door Daddy
*Her Baby Dreams
*The Cowboy Takes a Bride
*Texas Ranger Dad
*Small-Town Brides
  "A Mule Hollow Match"

*Lone Star Cinderella
*His Cowgirl Bride
†Her Forever Cowboy
†Cowboy for Keeps
Yukon Cowboy
†Yuletide Cowboy
**Her Rodeo Cowboy
**Her Lone Star Cowboy

*Mule Hollow
†Men of Mule Hollow
**Mule Hollow Homecoming

DEBRA CLOPTON

First published in 2005, Debra Clopton is an award-winning, multi-published novelist who has won a Booksellers Best Award, an Inspirational Readers' Choice Award, a Golden Quill, a *Cata-Romance* Reviewers' Choice Award, *RT Book Reviews* Book of the Year, and a Readers' Choice Award from Harlequin.com. She was also a 2004 finalist for the prestigious RWA Golden Heart, a triple finalist in the American Christian Fiction Writers Carol Award and most recently a finalist for the 2011 Gayle Wilson Award for Excellence.

Married for twenty-two blessed years to her high school sweetheart, Wayne Clopton, Debra was widowed in 2003. God's arms never let her or her two sons go during those dark months after Wayne's death. Her mission became showing the love she'd known through her characters and shining a light into readers' darkest hours with love and laughter in her books. Happily, in 2008, God led a couple of friends to play matchmaker and talk her into a blind date with Chuck Parks. Instantly hitting it off, Debra and Chuck were married in 2010 and are so thankful that God led them to each other.

They live in the country near Madisonville with Chuck's two high-school-aged sons. Debra has two adult sons, a lovely daughter-in-law and beautiful granddaughter—life is good! Her greatest awards are her family and spending time with them. You can reach Debra at P.O. Box 1125, Madisonville, Texas 77864 or at debraclopton.com.

Her Lone Star Cowboy
Debra Clopton

Love Inspired

Recycling programs
for this product may
not exist in your area.

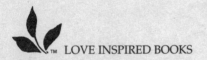 LOVE INSPIRED BOOKS

ISBN-13: 978-0-373-81612-5

HER LONE STAR COWBOY

www.LoveInspiredBooks.com

Printed in U.S.A.

Since ye have taken off your old self
with its practices and have put on the new self,
which is being renewed in knowledge
in the image of its Creator.
—*Colossians* 3:9–10

This book is dedicated to the real Montana Brown, the cutest little cowgirl around. Thank you and your wonderful parents for allowing me to use your name for my heroine in *Her Rodeo Cowboy* and as an ongoing character in the other two books in the Mule Hollow Homecoming series.

Though my heroine, Montana Brown, and her background are totally fictional, it was your love of all things cowgirl that inspired her creation in my mind. I knew when I met you that my character Lacy Brown had to have a cousin and her name had to be Montana....

For the real Montana Brown—may you always ride like the wind as you ride for the love of it! But most of all, always continue as you are now, riding for God who gave you your talent.

I'd also like to give a special shout-out to Libby Cannon and Lisa Webb! Anytime I have a rodeo or stock question, you friends are my go-to gals and I couldn't do it without you. Any mistakes are completely my fault! You girls do me proud every time.

And last, I want to thank veterinarian, Lisa VanReenen, for all of her expert, interesting and insightful help on toxic plants and ill cattle for this book! Because of you, Lisa, I have a plot twist I loved creating and I can also spot a toxic plant in seconds :) They're everywhere! This was really fun—and of course any and all mistakes would be totally mine...you are *awesome*.

Chapter One

Veterinary assistant Gabi Newberry pulled her light jacket tight, useless as it was against the rain. She huddled inside it and stared at the tire of the cattle trailer she'd been pulling behind the clinic's truck. Buried axle deep in thick clay mud, the trailer was sitting at a very risky angle. Grimacing, Gabi felt embarrassment creep up her skin as she studied her handiwork. What had she been thinking?

Susan Turner, her new boss and the local vet here in Mule Hollow, had asked Gabi if she was comfortable pulling a trailer. "Sure," Gabi had quipped with confidence. She was, but she hadn't planned on the torrential rain blowing in and crashing her party. What a mess.

The two black calves in the back of the small trailer bawled loudly, making her feel even worse. The poor animals were struggling to keep their balance in the precariously tipped trailer. Gabi empathized with them, having felt as if she'd been trying to do the same thing with her life, up until a few weeks ago.

"I'm sorry, little fellas—" she said, just as thunder boomed and lightning struck, far too close for comfort. At the same instant, a ferocious gust of wind whipped her baseball cap from her head! Gabi squealed and made a wild grab for the hat. A lost cause, she watched in dismay as it flew up and out of her reach, then dove dramatically, straight into the rushing water of the deep ditch beside her.

Watching how quickly the swift current swept her hat away sent a shiver of alarm running through Gabi. A few more feet and she'd have been in real trouble, with the trailer very likely tipping all the way over with the poor calves inside.

"This is bad," she muttered, her gut twisting with unease.

When she'd come back home to Mule Hollow, she hadn't expected to get caught in a flash flood her first week here. Her grandmother, Adela, would be worried about her out in this weather. Though she'd been raised till she was twelve near the Texas Hill Country, it had been thirteen years since she'd spent more than a week during the summer here. But still, she remembered how quickly flash flooding could happen and the dangers involved.

The sky had just been threatening rain when she'd headed out to return these calves to their owner less than an hour ago. Now it was almost black as the distant thunder clouds had taken a sudden swing in her direction. The lower peaks of the ominous clouds dipped in ice-cream-cone-shaped tags. Anyone in these parts knew that clearly spelled "tornado warning."

Without her hat Gabi's hair was drenched in seconds and rivulets of water washed down her face. Blinking, she studied the situation. There was no way she could get the trailer out by herself. Cellphone service was awful out here too, so calling for help wasn't an option. Bottom line—she was on her own.

Turning, she searched the horizon, squinting against the wind and rain pelting her face. Spying a rooftop in the distance, her heart jumped with a rush of hope.

It was pretty far off and the lightning was bad. Still, she knew despite the risk she needed to seek help there.

The only other choice though was to get in the truck and wait for someone to come by. With the calves bawling louder, Gabi stood there contemplating what to do. The situation was worsening by the second.

Her mouth went dry as panic crept over her. *Take action!*

She could not just sit there and wait for someone to come rescue her. Gabi pushed her hair out of her eyes and decided cutting cross-country to the house was her best chance.

Drenched from head to toe, she started toward the water. Then she hesitated. Should she let the calves out of the trailer? She decided getting back here with help was still her best possibility, and so she continued down to the edge of the rushing water.

Sticking her foot into the water, she braced herself then trudged forward. The water was higher than she'd realized, the ditch much deeper. Struggling against the rushing water, she managed to make it across without taking a plunge. Lightning exploded across the sky and thunder boomed just as she started up the incline—

The fierceness of it was startling and took Gabi's breath. She slipped and fell to her knees. Gasping, unable to catch her balance, she plunged straight toward the rushing water!

Jess Holden couldn't believe what he was seeing! The trailer was in a dangerous position, but it was the woman careening toward the rushing water that had him slamming on his brakes.

Bursting from his truck at a dead run, he slipped on the wet clay mud but held his balance as he went down on bent knee and skated the incline like a runner sliding feet first into home plate. She'd just started trying to regain her balance after hitting the water, but the current and the slick mud weren't cooperating. She lost her footing again and the water carried her swiftly downstream. Her head went under and her hands flailed above water. Jess staggered through the water after her, grabbed for her but missed. Diving for her again, he snagged the first thing he could reach—the collar of her shirt! Dragging her up out of the water, she coughed and sputtered, twisting around as her feet scrambled to find purchase in the muddy water.

"It's okay," he yelled over the wind. "I've got you." Holding his ground in the rising water, he seized her around the waist and hauled her up and out. Her feet came free of her boots as he slung her over his shoulder.

"What are you doing?" the woman sputtered. "Put me down. My boots!"

Concentrating on keeping them both upright, he held tight and turned back the way he'd come. "I'm saving you, lady, that's what I'm doing."

"But my boots. They're—" She struggled like a wildcat in a tote sack.

When he made it to the top of the muddy incline, he set her loose.

She immediately put distance between them. "I could have done that myself," she snapped, pushing a wild mass of wet hair out of her face. She had mud on her cheek that the rain quickly washed away.

"Are you kidding me? You weren't doing so well, and I wasn't taking any chances." Ignoring her anger, he turned his attention to the trailer and the unhappy animals staring at him.

"We need to get them out of here. What were you doing on the other side of that ditch anyway?" Jess asked, shaking his head.

"I was crossing the pasture to get help at that ranch, that's what." She waved a hand in the direction of the ridiculously distant house. "I couldn't get the trailer unstuck and I needed to get help for these little guys."

"Crossing a pasture during a thunderstorm like this—not smart," he scolded. "That trailer is down for the count right now." He strode toward his truck. The clueless woman trailed him.

"I know that. But I couldn't get it unstuck by myself. What should we do?"

The storm raged and he gauged the angry-looking sky. Flash flood and tornado warnings were in effect all over the area. "We're getting out of here. That's what."

Her eyes flared wide. "But you can't just leave them—" She stuck her hand on his chest.

He chuckled, despite the dire situation then, sidestepping her, he yanked open the back door of his double-cab truck. Quickly he flipped up his seats, then winked at the bedraggled gal as he backtracked past her in an attempt to ease her alarm. It was hard to tell what she really looked like with her hair being plastered to her face. Her big eyes widened at his wink.

"You're going to put them in there?" she asked, slipping and sliding to keep up with him.

"Yep, that's the plan," he drawled.

When he got the latch up on the trailer, she automatically grasped the door and held it open for him. Easing inside, careful not to slip, Jess grabbed the nearest calf and hoisted it into his arms.

After he got the first terrified calf in the truck, she was waiting at the trailer, ready to open the door for him when he went in for the second baby.

In a matter of minutes, working together they had both dripping-wet calves in the backseat area of his truck cab. Lightning crackled across the sky as they finally slid into the front seat and slammed the doors against the storm.

"I'm Jess Holden," he said the second they hit the road.

"I'm Gabi Newberry," she practically yelled over the wailing calves. "Thanks for coming along when you did."

Finally relaxing a bit, he shot her a grin. "You're welcome. But listen, the next time you get caught in the middle of a storm like this or even just a lightning storm, don't take off across open pasture. You were asking to get yourself killed back there." He'd lost his hat somewhere out in the storm so he took one hand off the wheel long enough to sweep his wet hair from his eyes.

Her big eyes narrowed as he glanced at her. He hadn't noticed before but they were a sharp, clear John Deere green and looked almost unreal as they caught the flash of lightning that lit the sky in front of them. Her skin was a soft gold, having gotten some color back after he had first snatched her from the water. She sort of resembled Gwyneth Paltrow. In short, wet hair and all, the woman sitting in the truck beside him was beautiful. Though the hike of her brow at the comment told him there was more spunk in those gentle features than met the eye.

"I wasn't getting killed," she denied, her spine stiffening. "I was getting help like I needed to."

"You were on a collision course with a lightning bolt, if you didn't drown before that."

He slid his gaze back toward the road, worried they might not make it back to the main road before the gravel washed away. Leaving them stranded out here.

He kept that bit of info to himself—no need to rile her up anymore.

She suddenly smiled. "You know what, you're right. I'm so glad you showed up when you did. God sent you along just at the right moment. Thank you, Jess Holden, my knight in shining armor."

Jess chuckled. He wasn't surprised by much, but she'd gotten him with her complete turnaround. "You're welcome. You're Adela's granddaughter, right?" He'd heard the fellas talking about her down at Sam's Diner. Adela Ledbetter Green was one of the older ladies in town. She was married to Sam who owned the local diner and there had been much excitement surrounding Adela's granddaughter coming to town.

"Yes, I am."

He grinned. "Seeing as how Adela is one of three older ladies known as the Matchmaking

Posse of Mule Hollow, do you know what you're getting yourself into by moving back here?"

They'd finally reached the blacktop and Jess breathed a little easier. He paused at the stop sign and studied his passenger, waiting for her to answer his question. He'd been holding off the matchmakers for a while, a bit startled that they hadn't tried harder to match him up with someone. Those three ladies had the "fix'n up" on the brain.

Gabi smiled, exposing a deep dimple. "Oh, I'm aware of what my grandmother does. But I already told her I was off-limits for now. Believe me, I'll be looking for a husband again— I mean, someday soon. But right now I just want to get settled." She cocked her wet head to the side, her gaze probing. "Do you know the Lord?"

Jess had been caught off guard by the "again" and then by her wanting to know if he knew the Lord. "Sure," he very nearly stammered, feeling a little uncomfortable. He and God knew each other, but they kept their distance.

"Oh, wonderful," she gushed, grinning, bright and beautiful. Her eyes warmed with joy. "Just wonderful! I gave my life to God about a month ago and I'm about to bust figuring out what He has in store for me."

Excitement radiated off Gabi like sunshine off new snow. It had Jess forgetting to press the gas pedal, leaving them sitting at the edge of the road. She winked at him—probably because his expression mirrored his surprise.

"I know, I know, I get a little excited over this. And I have to admit that getting stuck on the side of the road in tornado weather isn't exactly what I was expecting today. But you know what?—I think God must have meant for me to meet you today and that's what all of this is about. And if so, this craziness has been well worth everything."

"Thanks," he chuckled. The woman had an infectious way about her and he couldn't help the grin that lingered as he held her gaze. She was studying him like he was a painting on a wall or something. He lost his train of thought for a second and decided it was time to drive. He eased the truck onto the pavement. At last, after miles of soggy dirt road, he felt his wheels meet with solid ground. Feeling her gaze, he glanced at Gabi again and yup, she was studying him again.

"What's wrong?"

"Nothing's wrong." She sighed. "I'm just trying to figure out why God sent you into my life."

One thing was for certain, Gabi Newberry

was different. "That's easy enough," he teased, hiking a brow as he looked back at the road. "You obviously needed someone to rescue you from the water and tell you to stay out of the elements." He was only half joking.

"You're one of those men who has to be bossy, aren't you?" she asked, reaching to turn up the heat in the truck—since they were both soaked, it was a bit chilly in the cab.

"I'm just being honest."

She gave a short laugh. "You're being bossy. I wouldn't have drowned. I can swim like a fish."

The rain had slowed up to a drizzle and he could see a patch of sun peeking through the gray clouds. The lightning had moved farther off but still flashed in the distance over Gabi's shoulder. He glanced at her just as a flash sparked behind her. It mirrored the spark of challenge he saw in their green depths. "Um, you were drowning when I pulled you out. You risked your life when you should have been waiting for help."

"I did what I thought I needed to do. I couldn't just let these little guys stay out there and risk that trailer going over." As if knowing they were being discussed, the calves bawled louder and stuck their wet noses over the seat.

"Look, Gabi. I've just met you, but out of respect for your grandmother, I need to warn you to be more careful. You need to think smarter if you're going to be traipsing around out here in the country by yourself."

A calf poked its nose in her ear, causing her to laugh. She tucked her legs underneath her and turned to pet the calves that began trying to come over the seat. "You, Mr. Holden, are about as pushy as these boys. Thanks for your concern. I hear what you're saying, but I did what I had to do."

The vet clinic came into view. It was obvious that she was not going to take his advice to heart. Stubborn woman. "Next time you might not be so lucky." He pulled to a stop beside the holding pens behind the clinic.

Her gaze twinkled as she placed her hand on his arm. Her touch was warm and a spark of awareness danced along his skin. Her expression was a mixture of humor, laced with a firm you-aren't-going-to-tell-me-what-to-do attitude.

"So be it," she said, pulling away her hand and reaching for the door handle. "Thanks for the rescue and the ride."

"But *not* the advice," Jess said as he climbed out of the truck. He wasn't sure if the woman was soft on the brain, stubborn or both. Either way it was bothersome. He strode around to her side of the truck, where she waited with her hands on her narrow hips, her hair hung in tiny curls wisping about her forehead—they'd dried on the trip in and were a pale honey blond. His pulse kicked in abruptly, when she smiled that smile that lit across her face and let the dimple out of its hiding place.

"You can give me all the advice you want to. I'll consider it. I'll even thank you for it."

"But you won't take it. That's about what I'd expect." He opened the door and reached for the nearest calf.

Gabi already had the gate opened. She had a hand on her hip and one hand on the gate as he tramped past her. "Don't get comfortable thinking you know what to expect. I'm not as easy to read as you think I am, cowboy."

He paused to look down at her. She blinked innocently and her smile widened showing a bright white smile. There was nothing innocent in that smile. He had known her all of thirty minutes and he'd already figured her out. "I never said you were easy to read. Matter of fact, I have a feeling you probably work real hard at being complicated." He went for the other calf.

Gabi chuckled behind him. "You know what?"

He was walking past her with the other calf and paused to let it loose before facing her.

"What?" he asked, grinning because there was nothing else to do.

"I like you even if you are bossy. I'm going to have fun keeping you on your toes."

If he'd have had a hat, he'd have tipped it at her, but it was somewhere downstream stuck in the mud. Instead he just nodded. "Have at it. I like a woman who keeps me guessing."

"Then you're going to love me," she quipped, and strode toward the office.

Chapter Two

The jukebox was playing a lively country song when Gabi walked in the door of Sam's Diner after work. Immediately, the aroma of grilled steak and burgers had Gabi's stomach growling, reminding her that due to the wild day she'd had, she'd missed lunch. The scent of hot coffee pressed through the other unbelievably delicious scents and drew her gaze to the fresh pot of java sitting behind the counter.

"Gabi! Over here." Esther Mae Wilcox, her bright red hair bobbing, waved enthusiastically from the back booth. Her neon lime blouse was a splash of color against the backdrop of rustic wooden walls and oak booths.

Gabi said hello to a couple cowboys sitting at a table as she passed them. She'd helped administer vaccines to some cattle for them the day before. One of them had asked her out, and though she was officially unattached after her recent breakup with her fiancé, she was quick to thank him for the offer but told him she wasn't dating. He'd been cute when he'd proceeded to tease her that his heart was broken— it had been endearing actually, but nothing more. Where men were concerned she was a little numb, and she wasn't prepared to go there just yet. She had her life to get in order and her priorities figured out. One thing was certain, when she did start dating again, this time she knew the kind of man she wanted was the complete opposite of the one she'd chosen before.

Her number one priority when she looked for a husband this time was finding a man who loved the Lord as much as she did.

But for now, she was happy being here in Mule Hollow with her grandmother and her friends. They were going to help her become the kind of woman she wanted to be. Reaching the booth, Gabi hugged her grandmother, Adela, and her two friends Norma Sue Jenkins and Esther Mae Wilcox, before sitting in the empty seat beside Esther Mae. The three ladies were a contrast to each other. Esther Mae was as vibrant as her colored red hair, bright clothes and personality. Her Gram was a dainty, elegant lady with wispy white hair and a serene, fine-boned face that was dominated by electric blue eyes. Norma Sue was robust with wiry gray hair and a beaming smile.

"Sit down and tell us about this exciting day you've had."

Norma Sue's words startled Gabi.

"Don't look so surprised," Norma Sue continued. "News in a small town travels faster than a greased pig down a water slide."

"That's the truth," Esther Mae added. "We want all the details. Adela told us you got stuck this morning and that Jess Holden came to your rescue!"

Before Gabi could answer, the swinging doors of the kitchen opened and Sam came striding out, giving her a reprieve from further questions.

"Hey, Gabi girl," he called, his weathered face lit with a grin. A small man, built like a jockey, he moved with brisk intent. Snagging the coffee pot from the burner, he grabbed a cup in the other hand and strode, with his bow-legged gait, to the table and poured her a cup. "What were you a doin' out thar in the middle of a tornado anyway?" he asked, studying her sternly as he poured.

So much for a reprieve! Gabi realized she was in for it as all eyes zeroed in on her.

"It was tur-a-ble out thar. Jest tur-a-ble," Sam

continued, crossing his arms, letting the half-full coffee carafe dangle at his elbow.

"Terrible is the right word," Esther Mae gushed, turning in the booth seat so she was facing Gabi. "I'm so glad Jess found you. I can just see that handsome hunk of cowboy rushing in to pull you out of the raging waters. This would make a wonderful story for Molly's column."

"What!" Gabi gasped. She'd called Adela after she'd gotten back to the clinic, wanting to make sure Adela had made it through the storm okay, too. How did they know about Jess pulling her from the flooded ditch?

"You all right, thar?" Sam asked, patting her gently on the back.

A vivid image of an overblown story about her and Jess meeting in a violent storm with a tornado bearing down upon them popped into her imagination. Molly was a local writer who did a syndicated newspaper article about the little town, the cowboys and the matchmakers. It was hugely popular and she was a fan herself. But… "No—no article," she stuttered, choking on coffee. "Seriously—no."

Norma Sue hooted, slapping the table with her hand. "We're just having some fun with you."

"That's right," Esther Mae chuckled. "No

need to get all choked up. Who do you think we are?"

"The Matchmaking Posse, that's who!" Gabi blurted out. Squinting her eyes she gave them all a teasing, but firm warning. "Gram, please tell them I'm off the market."

"That's totally understandable after what you've been through," Adela said, her smile sympathetic.

"It sure is," Esther Mae cut in. "I can't believe that man broke up with you because of your faith."

"Hmmph," Norma Sue snorted. "You're better off without him."

"Unequally yoked isn't a good thing," Adela said. "God has plans for you with a good Christian man."

The conversation was bouncing around more than a pair of wet sneakers in a hot dryer. Unwanted, a sense of loss for Phillip stabbed Gabi's heart. Sadly though, Norma Sue was right. Six weeks ago she and her fiancé had called off their engagement after she'd given her life to the Lord. Looking back now, Gabi knew the relationship had been doomed in the first place. But still, she hadn't expected the man she'd *thought* she loved to leave her because he didn't care for her newfound faith. But then, she knew there was more to the story. More to it than the ladies or even her Gram knew.

A tight knot filled Gabi's chest. Her gaze dropped to her empty ring finger and the slow boil of anger and embarrassment bubbled inside of her. "Come on, y'all. You know I'm not here looking to build a relationship with a man. I'm here to build my relationship with God. I'm going to make up for lost time and try to make a difference in someone's life. I'm here to learn how to do that from y'all, not have y'all match me up with one of your cowboys." And work on herself—the Lord only knew she had a lot of work to do on herself.

"And God will use you," Adela assured her. "I'm so glad you're safe and you've at last made the decision to let Him be the Lord of your life."

"Me too," Gabi agreed, understanding how close she'd come to disaster—both with the car accident and her life in general. "Every time I think about slamming into that telephone pole and how totaled my car was." She paused, her heart catching. "I just can't believe I walked away with minor injuries."

It had been a horrible wreck…. Gabi pushed thoughts of it aside, not wanting to think on it.

"I agree," Esther Mae said, her glass of sweet tea paused in midair before taking a sip. "God's got a plan for you. He has a plan for everyone and I just love watching Him work."

"God still wants you ta use yor head, though. The next time a tornado is coming, you need ta not head out with a load of cattle," Sam continued admonishing her, not letting go of his role as her protector.

"Sam, I wasn't expecting that storm to blow this way."

"It wasn't supposed to." The frown deepened on his weathered face—Gabi was surprised that it could get any deeper. "Out here, you got ta remember that you jest never know. Like Jess said, ya need ta be more careful. And that means don't be trying to traipse off across a pasture in the middle of a lightning storm."

"*Jess* told you that?" She hadn't said anything to Adela about going across the ditch for help. What had the cowboy been saying? Sam's next sentence confirmed her suspicions.

"Yup, came in right after he'd dropped your truck and trailer off at the clinic. The boy was still wet."

Boy. Jess Holden was a man, not a boy—the fact distracted her for a moment. Over six feet tall, arms like iron and strength to carry her easily up the hill, heart-stoppingly blue eyes, square jaw, dark hair curling with the rain. There had been nothing about the handsome cowboy that reminded her of a boy. Jess's smile flashed across her mind's eye—okay, so he did have some boyish charm.

She was grateful to him for what he'd done, but coming in here and talking about it was not good. "What exactly did he say?"

Adela smiled gently and worry creased her eyes. "He said you were falling into the ditch full of raging water when he first saw you. That you got swept off your feet and towed underwater before he could get to you. Just a few more seconds and he might not have seen you fall in or go under. He was thankful, and so are we, that he'd managed to be there when he was. God's taking care of you again, my dear."

Good deed though it was, Gabi was having a hard time getting past the fact that Jess had been in the diner talking about rescuing her. Was he bragging? He hadn't really seemed the type.

What mattered to her was that he'd been telling details she'd rather have kept silent so as not to worry her Gram. There was no call for that. None at all. And it bothered Gabi more than he could possibly know. She'd put her Gram through enough worry over the years and was determined to protect her from any more. That meant not making her worry over Gabi's frustrations with the cowboy.

"Yes, Gram, you're right," she managed to say, trying to hide her displeasure at Jess, while also being truly grateful for God's protective hand being on her life. "God has had His hands full looking out for me."

It was so true. Gabi's life had spiraled out of control before she'd given her life to the Lord. The drinking and partying lifestyle she and her fiancé had been living had been an empty one. Even more empty than she'd realized. And then she'd almost had a head-on collision with an oncoming car. She was still so thankful to the nurse who'd shared her personal testimony with Gabi and awakened her to the dead-end path she was taking with her life.

"I'd have been all right, with or without Jess's help. Honestly, it wasn't as desperate as he's obviously made it sound."

Sam looked less than convinced. "Jess said you were in the water b'cause you were on yor way fer help *across* the pasture. Gabi girl, you might have made it out of the water, but nothing about any of that's smart. *Particularly,* traipsing in the middle of the worst electrical storm we've had this year."

Gabi took a slow, deep breath. "I was *fine.* I just did what I needed to do."

"I can take care of myself, too," Norma Sue drawled, jumping on the frown wagon with

Sam. "But sometimes that means staying inside where it's safe."

The conversation was going downhill. How had it changed from worrying about some kind of crazy, romantic setup from the posse, to them jumping on her about not being careful? "Sooo, how are the plans for the second homecoming rodeo going?" she asked, deciding it was time to change the subject. She'd come home to Mule Hollow to be closer to Gram and to start a new life here. Adjusting to this many people trying to give input into her life would take some getting used to.

To her relief, Sam headed off to check on the new cook he was training in the kitchen and the ladies launched into a discussion about the second of three rodeos the town was having over the summer. The rodeos were to draw crowds to the small town but also to honor people who'd once lived here. There was a hope that some of them might move back like Gabi had chosen to do.

She listened and prayed for patience and the ability to make good choices. It was embarrassing to her to review and see what a mess she'd made of her life. It was hard knowing she hadn't made good choices, but she was determined she was going to do better. Learning to trust herself was going to be hard on so many levels.

Learning to take advice was going to be even harder.

But she could do it.

She *would* do it.

God had given her a second chance and she wasn't about to waste it. She was determined to start making a difference in the world around her. She just had to take a deep breath and stop messing up.

Jess swiped his brow with the back of his hand. There were definitely no storm clouds on the horizon today, like there had been two days earlier when he'd pulled Gabi Newberry from the flood waters.

"They look good," he said, gazing from the new bunch of cattle he'd just bought and unloaded, to his older brother. They'd been working cattle in the heat all day and Luke looked as hot and sweaty as he was.

"Real good," Luke agreed, a satisfied gleam in his eyes. "With these added to the herd we're going to look pretty good come next year with calves. The ranch is doing great, Jess. If we get some nice, slow rain soon, we'll be perfect."

"Yeah, would be great." Jess patted his neck with his bandana.

"Now you and Colt just need to find someone to love and be loved by and get married." Though Luke was grinning, Jess knew how serious he was.

"Never thought I'd see the day, but you surprised us both and bite the bullet," Jess said and then smiled.

Luke looked at him, totally contented. "Montana makes me happy—I'm more alive than I ever was before meeting her. I want that for you. I never knew how it felt to have someone love me like she does. I know I sound sappy but it's true, Jess."

"Sap," Jess grunted and they both laughed, understanding where they'd once been and how far they'd come. He was glad for Luke. The three brothers' childhoods had been less than perfect and Luke was Jess's hero.

Only four years older than Jess when their mother had run off and left them to fend for themselves with their alcoholic father, Luke had taken on a man's responsibility at the age of fourteen. Jess owed him.

"You held us together all of our lives. Strong doesn't hold a candle to you, bro, so you can be as sappy as you want to be."

"Seriously, Jess, it's good to have Montana in my life. But I want this ranch and these cattle to mean as much to you and Colt as it does to me."

"We're in it with you, Luke. But you've always worried about us. Been responsible for us. We're better men because of it. You know that." No one really understood exactly how Luke had been there for them. No one understood how bad it had been.

"You know I'd do anything for you," Jess continued. "But when it comes to marriage, I have to go with my own plans. Luke—it's time for you to think about yourself now. Me and Colt, we're doing all right."

Luke had had visions of Jess and Colt with lots of kids. The ranch was to be the backdrop for a picture-perfect life he and his brothers hadn't known as kids. Problem was, Jess had gone along with his vision for years because he didn't want to tell Luke he had no desire for family, and wasn't certain he ever would. Some people weren't cut out for love and he was one of them.

He had commitment issues—no matter how hard Luke had tried to protect him, it still remained that his dad had been committed to a booze bottle and his mother had been committed to herself. True, he was surrounded by people in Mule Hollow who were committed to long and healthy relationships, but he didn't have their genes. He had Holden genes. He wished Luke the best. But Jess was better on his own.

He liked it that way.

He enjoyed his freedom and didn't plan on giving that up any time soon.

Not even for Luke.

"I'm just not sure I'm the commitment kind of guy," he said, though he knew deep down Luke got it. They both knew their childhoods played a significant role.

"*Yes,* you are, Jess. The day you find the right woman, you'll commit for life. No doubt about it. You finish what you start, Jess, you always have. You're too hardheaded not to and you've been that way ever since you were a little kid."

Jess shot his brother a half grin. "That's called survival skills."

Walking along the corral toward their trucks, Luke paused. "Yeah, but don't you forget that God promises He will make good from bad for those who love Him, and your life proves it. Colt's, too. I'm proud of both of you and day before yesterday, you made me real proud by helping out Adela's granddaughter."

Jess had thought about the feisty Gabi many times since then. He grinned, thinking about how she'd asked him about his relationship with God. He wondered if she asked everyone she met or if she had some kind of radar that zeroed in on trouble. Jess hadn't told her that he and God weren't on the best of terms right now. But still, he had thought of her often.

"She was in a bind," he said, not elaborating. "I'm glad I was there to help or it could have been worse."

"I'm glad you were there, too. But the thing is, you were there and without thinking about it, you committed yourself to seeing it through to the end. Sam told me yesterday that you went back there, pulled her truck and trailer out and then drove it to her. You didn't have to do that."

"Anybody would have done that. It was the right thing to do."

"Maybe and maybe not. Thing is, you did." He paused. "I hear she's single."

Here we go. "Yeah, I heard the same thing."

"You interested?"

Jess heard the hope in his brother's voice. "Maybe. We'll see. Honestly, she's the one who didn't seem too interested."

Luke pulled open his truck door. "There ya go, buddy. You can change her mind, if you want to. And I can tell you the casual thing is a dead end."

"Okay, man, back down. Right now I'm committed to a herd of ladies in the south pasture who are waiting on this hay."

Luke chuckled as he got in his truck and slammed the door. "Well, I've got a lady at home waiting on me and she's a whole lot prettier than any of those hairy gals you're heading out to see. Talk to you later." Luke grinned at him through the open window and as he backed up the truck he called, "Think about it, Jess. I'm praying for God to send you a woman."

Shaking his head, Jess headed out in his own truck to the cattle in the south pasture. He had work to do. While Luke was praying for God to send him a woman, he *needed* to pray for God to send some rain. Of course, Jess wasn't praying, he figured prayers didn't really matter that much. If God felt like answering a prayer, then God answered. Not before.

Jess had stopped asking for anything a long time ago.

Looking across the pasture, he turned up the radio and took in his surroundings. He loved it here on the ranch. Luke had gotten one thing totally right. And that was the fact that Jess liked having a place to call his own. This ranch filled a hole in his heart, eased an ache he'd had for as long as he could remember. Here on this ranch, he was happy and content. He wasn't sure he'd ever risk that by getting married.

He'd do anything for Luke, but get married…
Couldn't do it.

Topping the ridge of a low hill, his attention was snagged by a group of buzzards circling in the pale blue sky.

Something was dead. Buzzards were a common sight here in the country, but Jess always checked it out when he was looking after the cattle. Driving toward the next ridge, he scanned the pastureland stretched before him. It was dry, not much grasslands left, thus the hay and feed they were having to put out, but it was still pretty land they'd bought.

The herd of Angus cattle grazed near a pond that was two feet low of water even after the rain they'd had two days before.

Topping the second hill, the pasture came into view.

Jess's gaze zeroed in on the heifer laying halfway down the hillside. His heart sank. Dead cattle were expensive and a threat to the entire herd.

There was no mistaking this heifer had been dead for some time. Hanging his head for a brief moment, he looked up and scanned the pasture. In the distance he was certain he spotted a second large mound that would be another heifer.

Not good. Not good at all.

Chapter Three

Gabi drove the truck over the cattle guard of Jess Holden's ranch. He'd found four dead heifers the evening before. Four at one time. They'd been dead too long for a necropsy to determine the cause of death, so her boss Susan sent her out to draw blood. For some reason, the idea of seeing the cowboy again caused a nervousness to wash over her.

Susan had confided to her that Jess and his two brothers had worked hard to scrape together the money to buy their ranch and stock it. The potential for these deaths to be something that could affect their entire herd had to be worrying them. Maybe make or break them.

Gabi hated to hear that. She was still thinking about it as the corral and Jess came into view. She would have been lying if she denied that she wasn't curious about the cowboy.

Standing beside the corral at the corner of the pasture, he watched her pull to a halt, his face a work of seriousness. The man was better looking than she remembered—if that were even possible. How in the world this guy was still walking around single in a town that had gone wild with matchmaking was a huge mystery. His hair was just the length to make a woman want to run her fingers through it, tucking it behind his ear. On some guys she might have thought it scruffy looking, but not on Jess. Nope. On him it looked great. It looked right—

What are you doing?

Surprised that she was thinking about Jess more intimately than she wanted to, Gabi shook her head. She'd just broken up with her fiancé a month ago. This proved what she'd realized earlier—she hadn't truly been in love with Phillip. Still, she was shocked by how swiftly she could become attracted to someone else.

Not just someone—Jess Holden.

Parking the truck she hopped from the cab, all business. She'd come to do her job. She didn't want his cattle to get all sick and die, but she didn't want to marry the guy, either—Gabi tripped at the thought, snagging her boot toe and nearly taking a dive at his feet.

"Watch it." Jess caught her arm. "Are you all right?"

"Oh yeah, I'm just a tripper." Her voice shook as she tugged away her arm from his warm grasp.

He chuckled. "So that's what happened the other day."

She made a face at him.

"Where's Susan?" he asked, his gaze flitting past her to the truck.

"She sent me on ahead to draw some blood for testing so the labs could get it started."

A brief hint of worry flashed across his expression. She knew he'd have rather Susan had showed up.

"That sounds like a good plan," he said, hiding his disappointment. "I pulled the cattle I think we should look at. They're in the corral."

Gabi didn't normally let negative reactions bother her, especially in such a stressful situation like this. After all the man was worried about his cattle. She followed him to the corral, a little stunned by how his reactions were affecting her. But she tried hard not to take it personally.

Jess had searched the property for any other sick or dead cattle and had found four total. He was worried. Everything they had was invested in this land, these cattle and the livestock. He owned his cattle rig outright but that was about the only thing the bank didn't actually own.

"Is this all of them?" Gabi asked surveying the ten cows.

"So far. I watched them this morning, trying to pick out any that might even look slightly ill."

Gabi stood quietly and observed them milling around. Her gaze skimmed the animals, lingering here and there. "They do look a little distressed. Not only their nasal activity, but some of them are drawn-looking in their stomachs."

"Yeah, they were sluggish about eating."

She glanced his way, her sparkling green eyes lit with agreement. "When stock is slow to eat, they're sick. Problem is, how sick? Let me grab my bag and we'll get to work. The quicker my part is done, the sooner Susan can give you answers."

"I'll have one in by the squeeze chute by the time you're ready."

"Sounds good." She paused after taking a couple steps and glanced at him over her shoulder. "We're going to figure this out, Jess."

She gave him a reassuring smile before continuing toward the truck for her equipment. He opened the gate and entered the pen with the cattle. It didn't take him but a few minutes to cull one from the bunch and herd him into the alley that led to the steel squeeze chute. He'd just pulled the lever that brought the bars in close, holding the heifer in place so that Gabi could draw the blood.

"You're quick," she said, striding to the pen.

"I should be," he said. "I do this every day." As worried about his livestock as he was, he couldn't help noticing that she looked as sunny and bright as a fresh summer day. She wore old jeans and scuffed boots that looked like they'd seen a lot of miles. Her tank top was bright pink and fresh looking and showed off her sun-kissed arms. She'd pulled her hair back into a ponytail with a bright yellow ribbon that fluttered in the warm breeze. He watched as she pulled out the syringe and prepared to take the first sample with speedy efficiency. "You look pretty quick yourself."

"I should be. I do this every day," she copied him and smiled through the steel bars before inserting the needle in the heifer's neck.

The animal hardly reacted to her expert touch. For some reason he'd had visions of Gabi making the animals nervous.

"You know, I'm mad at you." She didn't look up as she spoke.

"About what?"

She met his curious stare with frank eyes. "You *bragged* in the diner about rescuing me from that rushing water."

"I wasn't bragging. Sam asked why I was dripping water on his wood floors so I told him. There was no bragging involved. Concern? Yeah. Bragging? No way."

"You worried my grandmother for no reason."

He hadn't thought of that. "I told them you were safe." The cute quirk of her left eyebrow told him she was mad at him. Not to mention the green flash of fire in her eyes.

"You didn't have to tell them the details. You should have known it would cause Adela to worry." She pushed hard on the steel lever, releasing the heifer.

Jess let the next one into the chute. "She seemed fine to me. You're getting all bent out of shape for nothing."

"You think? My gram was worried and there was no need in it."

He thought about it for a minute. He hadn't called Colt or Luke and told them about the dead heifers or about the cattle that were looking ill. Why hadn't he? Because he didn't want to worry them. "I'm sorry," he said. "I didn't think."

She met his gaze through the bars. "It's just

that I've worried her enough in my lifetime. I'd rather not do that anymore."

There was a long silence as they worked together. He wondered what she'd done to make Adela worry. If she was prone to traipsing across pastures during electrical storms, then he could understand why. "I'm sure you didn't worry her too much," he said, unable to let her comment linger in the air.

Pulling more blood into the syringe, she frowned. "Sadly, I did. Anyway, I guess in some way all kids worry their parents and grandparents. Still, I don't want to cause Adela any more worry."

Jess could have told her that that wasn't necessarily true. Parents had to care before they could be worried. "You are lucky to have Adela in your life."

She yanked the lever again, releasing another heifer. "I'm not lucky. I'm blessed. God did right by me when He gave me my mother and my grandmother."

Growing up, Jess had watched other kids with parents who cared. He'd wondered what that would feel like.

"I know Miss Adela is a good woman, I'm sure your mother is too," he said, as they continued working through the cattle. She smiled, just enough to show a bit of the dimple that he'd seen during the storm.

"You know what my goal is now?" Light seemed drawn to her, making her blond ponytail sparkle and her suntanned skin glow.

"What?"

"I want to be a blessing to my Gram and anyone else who I meet. I'm not sure I can do it, but I'm trying." She finished pulling the blood. "You know what I mean?" Sincerity vibrated in her voice as she pulled the lever and let the last animal run free.

Jess hadn't ever thought about being a blessing to anyone. Looking at her, he almost wished he could say he knew exactly what she meant. But that wasn't true. "No. I don't know what you mean," he said, his brows crunching slightly as he spoke. "But, I can tell you that if that blood work comes back clear, you'll have been a big blessing to me."

She smiled a dazzler of a smile that blew his boots off.

"I hope so." She picked up the case full of blood samples and headed toward her truck. He closed the gate behind him and followed her, watching as she set them in the seat.

"Let's pray that this report comes back and it's an easy fix, or better yet that nothing is wrong with these heifers," she said turning back to him and holding her hand out toward him.

"That'd be great," he said, not sure what she was doing.

She cocked her head slightly then wiggled her fingers. "Hold my hand."

Jess was by no means a fool. He wasn't about to forego holding the hand of a beautiful woman. When he took her hand, his pulse kicked up a notch....

"Let's pray." She bowed her head.

Pray? Now?

"Oh, Father," she prayed, squeezing his hand in hers. "Please watch over Jess's cattle and let them stay healthy and strong. If they are ill, we pray You'll lead us to the answer quickly and that You'll help us to know what to do for them so that they return to health quickly. We ask in Your name that Your will be done. Amen."

Jess wasn't surprised by much, but this was twice that Gabi Newberry had done it. First asking about his salvation and now taking his hand and praying out loud—he wasn't sure which had him most startled. He was staring at the top of her head as she finished and raised happy eyes to his. She took his breath away.

"There that should do it." She grinned, squeezing his hand before letting go and stepping away from him. "I'm heading back so

I can get these samples to Susan. We should know something soon."

"Great," Jess said, still reeling from her prayer and the touch of her hand. He'd felt a wave of awareness the instant her hand had touched his.

Gabi Newberry had the ability to catch him off guard when most didn't. He liked that, but she also had a close relationship with the Lord. He wasn't used to that. Even Luke, who had a strong faith, didn't pray out loud unless it was before a meal. Jess didn't pray. He'd stopped a long time ago.

And he was fine with that.

Luke and several of his friends never gave up though. They asked him to come to church all the time. And every once in a while he went so they would feel better. But it didn't feel right to him, knowing how much resentment about his past he had buried inside of him. He didn't let his past affect him in many ways, but church was a hard fit.

Attractive to him as she was, Gabi's front-and-center faith had him backtracking.

Besides, he had a gut feeling that once she found out he wasn't sold on Jesus like she was, two things could happen. One, she'd want nothing to do with him even if she was attracted to him. Or two, she would make him her project, deciding she needed to "fix" him.

He was fine the way he was and didn't need, or want to be, fixed! Nope, that idea didn't sit well at all. Matter of fact, Jess figured the best course of action would be to steer clear of Gabi altogether, which was one more good reason to hope his cattle hadn't contracted anything that would require a lot of interaction with the vet clinic—or Gabi.

He needed favorable test results. He did *not* need Gabi out here testing cattle, drawing blood or trying to help him in any way.

Watching her drive off, he felt a pang of regret…she was like a ray of sunshine. Even mad at him. That made him smile.

Yup. He needed healthy cattle.

And he needed to steer clear of Gabi Newberry.

"I think it's a plant."

"A plant?" Gabi was changing the dressing on Peanut's wound when Susan came through the swinging door from the front of the clinic. Despite the painful wound, the colt was doing great. It wasn't every animal that would allow people to touch it after experiencing such a traumatic injury. Especially a vicious attack like Peanut had endured. "That could be good or bad. What are your thoughts?"

Gabi ran a gentle hand along Peanut's flank before stepping out of the stall. She'd had Jess on her mind more than she'd wanted to. She'd been worrying about him and his ranch—after what Susan had told her, Gabi couldn't stand the thought of something bad being wrong with his cattle and them all dying and leaving him and his brothers in a financial bind. She'd tried to be mad at him when she'd gone to take the blood samples, but she'd been unable to maintain her ire.

Goodness, when the man turned those silky brown eyes on her, it was kinda hard to stay mad. It was maddening, really.

Susan crossed her arms and leaned against the stall gate, checking out the colt's condition as she spoke. "I found that the liver values showed there was damage. I'm fairly certain that's what it is. But we both know that I can't be sure what kind of plant specifically without seeing the contents of the dead animal's stomach. That'll show what the cattle have eaten, and we can quickly get to the bottom of this if we got there in time. We don't want any more of Jess's livestock to die, so we are going to pray that we're able to locate the plant culprit and solve the issue before any more life is lost."

Just as Gabi had thought! "I agree," she said, hoping on the one hand she'd be sent to test, and on the other hand wishing she wouldn't. "So do you need me to find it?" she asked. There was no way Susan had time to traipse about Jess's pasture in search of a poisonous plant. The array of deadly plants and weeds was big, especially in drought conditions when weeds tended to pop up and good grasses were eaten down. It could be something hard to find. Plus, Susan knew Gabi had experience with this.

Susan nodded. "That's exactly what I need you to do. So grab a sample box and get out there to Jess's pastures and find any poisonous plant you can."

Hope and purpose filled Gabi—and yes, anticipation of seeing Jess Holden again. But she had a job to do and if she did it well, she might be able to prevent any more of Jess's cattle from dying. "I'll get right to it!"

"Love your attitude," Susan said, heading back toward the office. "I'll contact Jess and tell him you're heading his way. I know he'll be excited."

Gabi laughed because she wasn't so sure about that. She was fairly certain Jess would rather have Susan on the case, but hopefully he'd trust Gabi enough to give her a chance.

She ignored the excitement she felt at seeing him again. She was going to have to get a cap on that unwanted emotion. She was here in Mule Hollow to draw closer to God, and that had nothing whatsoever to do with a man. She was excited about getting to be a blessing to someone, anyone. That someone might just be Jess Holden.

Chapter Four

"There's some." Gabi pointed from the seat of his truck the a small patch of purple flowering weeds.

"Vetch," Jess said, shocked she was pointing at the very common weed here in Texas pastures. The list of plants that could have killed the heifers was long, but her pointing to vetch took him by surprise, as did her excitement about looking for poisonous plants on his ranch. He'd welcomed her enthusiasm for finding the plant that might be responsible for the death of his heifers. The woman had been hard at it from the moment she'd driven up. He was glad for the help but trying not to let his thoughts linger too long on how cute she was. She was there to help him out. And he was glad of it. But this? Vetch? It was everywhere. If it was poisonous, then he felt pretty stupid.

"Yes, hairy vetch is a very poisonous plant when it wants to be."

"Seriously? I've never heard of vetch killing cattle. It's a good, nutritious feed source."

"Most of the time it's a great food source. Stop here and let me get a sample. See, vetch is a real tricky little plant. You can graze cattle on it forever and never have a problem and then one day, boom—you've got sick cattle. Dead cattle."

"How have I not known this?"

She laughed. "You aren't stupid. It's a sneaky plant. It also just affects dark-skinned animals, like your Angus and Angus mixes."

"That's weird. What does it do?"

"It causes skin lesions around the head and the neck area, and also the tailhead."

"I didn't notice that on the heifers that died."

"I didn't notice it on any of the cattle you brought up for testing either. This is definitely not your culprit. But I'm getting samples of everything I see. Who knows, we could be surprised. There are some worse symptoms from vetch that you would have noticed, far more obvious alerts that something was wrong."

Floored, Jess listened to her finish talking about the symptoms this plant could cause in his cattle. He had to admit that he was impressed. She knew her stuff.

Full speed ahead, she hopped from the truck and took some plastic baggies with her. He followed, watching as she snipped different plants and placed them in bags. Hands on his hips, he stared at his pasture with renewed wariness and wondered what other toxic plants he might be harboring right beneath his nose that he was clueless about.

"Stop feeling bad about not realizing vetch is a toxic plant," Gabi said, reading his mind as she squinted up at him in the late afternoon sun. "There's only about a hundred known toxic plants in Texas alone. It's not like you'd know them all. And, believe me, you'd be surprised by some of them. Some ranchers know a few, but honestly, not many ranchers would know them all. That's what makes this so difficult. Some mimic others and some are toxic only under certain conditions."

She was close enough that he could see the tiny iridescent dark blue specks rimming her sparkling green eyes. Her eyes were incredible. He couldn't stop staring. This need to look at Gabi Newberry had to be curbed.

"How did you get to be so smart?" *Lame question, Holden.* "Did they teach you that in tech school?"

"Are you kidding? Susan's the vet, and even

she has to pull out books and do a search to figure out which one it could be."

"So what you're telling me is you're extremely smart and you just know all this stuff about toxic plants that you've been rattling off to me." That got him a big laugh and a wave of her blunt-cut nails.

"*No,* no. I'm no brain. Me, I'm an in-the-trenches kinda gal. You know, I have to do the grunt work, get my hands dirty and learn things that way."

That made him smile. "So how *do* you know this?"

She shrugged. "One of the places I worked my first year on the job had a major problem. Cattle were dropping left and right. It was a terrible thing. It took us weeks and a ton of dead livestock before we found out what the problem was. Turned out it was a combination of two things, not just toxic plants. That was what had everyone turned around so we couldn't figure it out. Plain bad coincidence that there was a fungus in the feed they were buying and a Tarweed plant problem at the same time."

"So you spent a lot of hours in the pastures taking samples."

"You got it. And more time pouring through books and on the internet researching symptoms. Plants are really, really hard to diagnose.

That's why Susan thought I could at least come on out to see what the obvious plants could be that might be your problem. Not super smart, just super tenacious. I don't tend to give up if I'm on a project."

"I'm impressed."

"Don't be. Not one thing here to be impressed about. I'm a fairly stupid person. My past speaks loud and clear."

That made him even more curious about her past, but he didn't pry. "I am impressed and grateful too for your help. If it had been one cow, it could have been anything. But four at one time worries me that they could all drop dead by morning."

"Then let's get busy. Show me where the cows were found and let's search those areas first. Chances are if it was toxic plants, the poisoning happened over a period of time. But it also could have been almost immediate. If so, we are on a race against time. Who knows, maybe we'll catch a break and figure it out immediately."

Jess had a bad feeling that wasn't going to happen as he led the way back to the truck and they headed toward the pasture where he'd found the dead cattle.

Soon as he stopped, Gabi went to work. He

tagged along beside her. They talked plants for a while and then took some samples.

"Why did you decide to move here?" Jess asked, filling the silence that settled between them when they were again in the truck. He glanced at her as he drove through one gate toward the back pasture where the cattle had been grazing.

"To be near my Gram. And God. Oh, wow, do I have a lot of catching up to do between me and God. And that is what I'm here for. Tell me about you, Jess," she said, looking serious. "You and your brothers own this wonderful place. So you ranch all the time?"

"This ranch is what I do with my brothers. My business is I buy and transport cattle for myself and others. That income supplements this ranch. The same goes for Luke. He has his rodeo stock. I'm just as worried about his stock as I am our cattle. He's got a full schedule lined up for them and if we've got something infectious going on, then this isn't good."

"I'm trying to be positive here, but truth is either way it could be bad." She didn't mince words, he liked that, but she gave him a reassuring smile. "On the other hand, it could also be okay. And we know that. So let's concentrate on figuring this out. The rodeo stock is kept separate from your livestock, right?"

"Right." He pulled the truck to a stop where another one of the cows had been found.

"It's not going to be bad. God's going to come through on this. We just have to do our part to figure it out. Right?"

Jess didn't answer her question as she hopped from the truck. Pausing with her hand on the door, she cocked her head to the side. "Right?" she clarified. "You do believe that God's got this figured out, don't you?"

Jess frowned, not exactly sure how to answer the perky vet tech. When was the last time God ever took care of anything where he was concerned? Unfortunately, that wasn't exactly the answer a newfound Christian gal with an enthusiastic heart for God wanted to hear. So, he kept his mouth shut.

Saturday evening Gabi went to Bible study at Norma Sue's. Gram was there, plus Esther Mae and several couples around her age. She knew many of them from her visits, but there were several that had moved to Mule Hollow who she didn't know. A really sweet couple sat beside her. Stacy and Emmitt were shy but nice. Roy Don, Norma Sue's husband led the study on being a good steward with your life. That really hit home for Gabi, since she was trying hard to be responsible. Attending Bible study on a Saturday night was a big step—it was certainly different from hitting the bars and waking up with a booming headache.

Yes, life was different.

Life was better.

She thought about her friends back in Austin who she and Phillip had hung out with almost every night. Most of them had been musicians like Phillip, playing hard both on stage and off. Not all of them were out of control. Some of them were responsible and knew when to say no to another drink. She hadn't been one of them. And it had really scared her. If she hadn't woke up when she did, giving up alcohol wouldn't have been as easy. Without God's help, she wasn't sure if she could have at all. There wasn't a day that went by that she didn't think about it. Keeping busy and studying the Bible was helping.

She listened intently as different people talked about what they'd done to use God's gifts in their lives responsibly. She took mental notes and kept her mouth shut. She hadn't talked to anyone about her past, and she didn't plan on doing it any time soon. She didn't feel like opening up about all of her mistakes. Talk about embarrassing. Sure, she'd insinuated a few things to Jess about her life. But then she'd caught herself and hadn't revealed too much.

Nothing about how really out of control she'd been…what would people think of her if they knew?

Nope, she was here to move forward. Not to look back and be judged by her past.

There was nothing wrong with a girl wanting her privacy. Nothing at all.

Chapter Five

Sunday morning brought a big smile to Gabi's heart as she rolled over in bed and stared out the window from her room in Gram's house. Breathing in the scent of lemon wax and rose petals, she stretched slowly, taking advantage of the last few minutes before she sprang out of bed.

When Gram had married Sam she'd chosen to move from the small house she'd lived in for years, which happened to be beside the large family home that Adela had grown up in. She'd turned that spacious treasure into an apartment house. The grand old house sat on Main Street at the entrance of town with its wide porches, majestic turrets and many, many memories from Gabi's childhood. It was here that her faith had been grounded by both Gram and her mother. She'd no excuse for turning her back on God.

Beside it, though she'd moved to Sam's home in the country, Adela had kept her small home—just in case family came to visit or wanted to move home. She'd insisted that Gabi live here. Staring out the window, Gabi could see a red bird sitting on the rain gutter. Joy filled her. She loved her life and was so thankful just to be living the opportunity she'd been given. She was home in so many ways than the obvious.

She dressed quickly, yanking on an old pair of jeans and an oversized green T-shirt. She tugged her boots on, then headed out the door. She had animals to tend at the clinic before getting ready for church.

The clinic was quiet as she unlocked the door and entered. From the back, the colt nickered. Knowing she was going to help the hurting animal renewed Gabi's certainty that she was doing what she was supposed to do with her life.

"Hey, Peanut," she said, softly. He ambled up and watched her open the gate and enter his stall. Gabi ran her hand over the silken star on his forehead, enjoying the trust in his eyes.

"You're going to be okay, boy," she assured him, then gently she began cleaning his wound. She loved that she could help hurting animals heal. She also liked knowing she could help animal owners too…. Jess came instantly to mind.

The handsome cowboy had been in her thoughts all night. Even after she'd left the ranch, she'd spent time digging through her book of toxic plants. But that wasn't the one thing she was thinking about. It was his reaction to her talking about God.

He'd sidestepped her attempt at getting him to agree that God had the situation under control. She was certain he'd purposefully began talking about plants in order to not talk about God. Why?

Peanut flinched as she rubbed salve on his wound. "Sorry, fella," she apologized. "Why wouldn't Jess want to talk about God, huh, Peanut? I mean, ever since asking God into my life, I like to talk about Him." It was a relationship and she wanted to get closer to Him.

After she finished with the colt, she checked the other patients then hurried back home, showered and dressed. There were several groups of people standing around on the grass in front of the white plank building when Gabi arrived at the Mule Hollow Church of Faith. She loved the steep rooftop and tall white steeple of the church. Though it was a typical country church, it had stood the test of time well. There could be no doubt in anyone's mind that this house of God was well cared for and had been built on a solid foundation. Just looking at it gave Gabi a sense of peace and excitement at the same time. She had a smile on her face as she hurried from her old truck and headed toward her friends.

Life was good. How could it get any better?

"Ain't you a pretty sight this morning," Applegate Thornton boomed, loud enough for everyone within a mile radius to hear. Skinny as a man could be and not break in half, his seemingly perpetual frown lifted in a smile.

Gabi beamed at his good-natured greeting. "Why, thank you, Mr. Applegate." She'd pulled on a white blouse and a red skirt with white sandals and was feeling fresh and summery. After wearing jeans and boots at work all week, it was fun to be a little girly. "Even a tomboy like me enjoys frilling up at least once a week."

"You done good," Stanley Orr added, almost as loud as his buddy App. His cherry cheeks beamed. The two men were in their late seventies, hard of hearing and retired. They could be found most mornings frowning over a game of checkers at Sam's Diner. Gabi usually saw them when she stopped in for her morning coffee. She enjoyed giving them a hard time and they relished throwing it right back at her and everyone else who stopped in. They were certainly part of Mule Hollow's charm.

Before she could say more, Esther Mae and Norma Sue hurried over.

"That's some hat, Esther Mae." Gabi was unable to take her eyes off the multicolored monstrosity. There were feathers and flowers erupting all over the place. It looked like a flower arrangement that had had a head-on collision with several flocks of birds.

"Thank you. Joseph had a coat of many colors and *I* have a hat of many colors. Don't you just love it!"

Norma Sue grunted. "If Joseph's coat was as gosh-awful as that hat, then it's no wonder his brothers sold him off to Egypt. Just shows you that God will use anything to accomplish His will."

Esther Mae harrumphed and hiked her chin in the air. "They were jealous of his coat." She patted her feathers and gave her friend a teasing grin. "You can't have it, Norma Sue, get your own."

"My own! We can only hope it's one of a kind."

Gabi laughed, "Y'all never stop."

"Ain't that the truth," App boomed. Giving them a sour look, he shook his head then addressed Gabi again. "I was about ta ask you—

before we were interrupted." He gave them another hard look for good measure. "What'd ya find out at Jess's place yesterday about his cattle?"

"That's what we came to ask about, too," Esther Mae said, turning serious. "Did you find a poisonous plant killing all his cattle?"

News sure did travel fast. She hadn't told her Gram, so how had they all found out about this? "I was just out there looking—and before y'all get all up in a tizzy, it was only four heifers."

Stanley looked shocked. "Four's enough, but I heard it was more on the lines of ten."

"I don't know where you're getting your information but it was only four."

"For now," App said, sounding dire. "I shor hope you find the plant."

"We don't know for certain that it is a plant. Susan suspects it from the blood work she's seen, and wanted me to get more information on it."

That had them all bursting into advice on the various toxic plants that they were aware of in the county. Several other people stopped by to join in on the conversation. Gabi listened, taking in every bit of knowledge she could gleam from the folks who knew this area best. It was not to be taken lightly.

They were all talking when suddenly Norma Sue elbowed Esther Mae so hard her hat slid forward. She nodded toward the parking lot and everyone, including Gabi, turned to see what had Norma Sue's mouth hanging open. It was Jess.

Half the front lawn of the church turned to look at Jess as he walked across the parking lot. Glancing at his watch, he knew he'd hit the time between Sunday school and church services. Normally when he came, he timed it so he got there right before Adela started playing the piano and everyone was already inside the church. Today he'd rushed it just a little.

His gaze was drawn instantly to Gabi standing among the group. Her blond hair sparkled in the sun like it always did. It was the first time he'd seen it hanging free of the ponytail she usually wore and it *really* caught the sun this way. She was in a skirt. It was red, and swung around her calves, very feminine. He had half expected her to be in her jeans, and was surprised and pleased to see her like this. And that was the reason he was about to get himself in trouble. Because half the congregation knew what had brought him out this morning. That was the reason, instead of going into the sanctuary when Adela had clearly begun to play the piano, they were still watching him.

He was asking for trouble, stirring up talk by showing up at church for the first time all summer. They all knew why he'd come.

God was probably not too pleased knowing he'd come to see Gabi instead of Him. But the truth was, Jess had stopped caring a long time ago whether God was happy with him or not.

He didn't let that mess up his life or anything. He was pretty happy for a thirty-year-old guy. He'd made a good life for himself, despite not having parents worth a dime and a "Heavenly Father" who'd abandoned him right along with them.

Nope, he'd come to church to see Gabi even though he'd tried hard to talk himself out of it. The problem was Gabi Newberry thought God walked on water. She had a shiny, untarnished view of how God was interested in a personal relationship with her and everyone around her. She'd tried hard to talk to him about it yesterday. That should have sent him running from Gabi.

But no, here he was, walking into church, stirring up matchmaking talk. And for what?

He knew God wasn't interested in a relationship with everyone. He knew this from hard, firsthand knowledge and he also knew there

was no way he was going to be the one to tell
this to Gabi. He wasn't about to be the one to
take that shine out of her eyes. That shine was
what drew him.

That shine was the thing that kept nagging at
him long after she was gone. Thing was, Gabi
Newberry had something he wanted. And try
as he might to talk himself out of it, he'd put
on his starched shirt and jeans and was delib-
erately walking into trouble.

It was a completely crazy move.

Chapter Six

"Mornin'," Jess drawled, tipping his Stetson as he came to a halt in front of Gabi.

The man looked like he'd just stepped off the cover of some glossy cowboy magazine, all spruced up and spit-shined, as her grandfather would have said. And oh how nice and shiny he was!

Gabi felt a nudge in the small of her back from either Esther Mae or Norma Sue.

Everyone but her gave him a response but she was still tongue-tied. It was totally messing with her mind the way those beautiful teal eyes were looking at her.

She forced her throat to work. She wasn't going to look like a ninny in front of everyone. "Mornin' to you, too. I wasn't expecting to see you here."

"We weren't, either," Norma Sue added,

shooting straight to the point. "But it sure is good to see you!" She grabbed him in a bear hug that had Jess looking embarrassed.

"Um, thanks, Norma Sue. I'm glad to see you, too."

"Me too," Esther Mae said patting his bicep. She looked at Gabi. "Isn't he a handsome fella? I just love his hair."

"The handsomest," Gabi agreed, wanting to laugh when his eyes almost rolled. It was obvious he would rather be walking over hot coals than standing here being fussed over. But she liked the way he stood patiently and let the matchmakers get all gooey over him. He was really adorable, even though she could tell he'd rather be somewhere else. "And he has such a wonderful disposition. Don't y'all agree?"

"My disposition is thinning by the moment."

That made them all laugh.

"Come on," Norma Sue chuckled. "We're all about to be late. Adela's gonna hit the last stanza of "Standing on the Promises" and everyone's going to be sittin' on the premises before we're even in there."

App, who'd headed in earlier to man his post at the front doors, poked his head out about that time and glared, waving his hand at them to come in.

"There's the signal," Esther Mae chuckled.

Norma Sue led the way, shaking her head. "How that man got the position as greeter is beyond me."

"I think I'm gonna hug App," Jess whispered in Gabi's ear, falling into step beside her.

"It's about time," App hissed, causing half the church to turn and see what he was talking about.

Gabi would have laughed, but she was walking into the building beside Jess and all eyes were focused on them. She came to a screeching halt. Jess bumped into her and she thought she heard him groan. Esther Mae and Norma Sue had left her high and dry. They'd entered ahead of her and were rushing the choir loft like two linebackers. Where to sit, she wondered, looking at App. He hiked a bushy brow and gave her another grin that had her nervous.

"You two follow me," he commanded and led her and Jess to a pew three rows from the back.

As they squeezed into the nearly full pew, Gabi groaned this time. She'd come to church to worship, not think about a good-looking cowboy whose elbow was rubbing up against hers in the crowded pew.

That was distracting…but it wasn't going to work.

No sir, her head was not that easily fooled... well, not anymore anyway.

She reached for a hymnal, determined to be unaffected by Jess. She was helping the man hunt for toxic plants and that was that.

Jess reached for the book the same time she did. "Sorry," she whispered, drawing back her hand.

He smiled, and her stomach went all fluttery. This was not going to be easy.

"Colt, congratulations. You make us proud, bro."

"Thanks," Colt's voice crackled over the bad connection. "I try anyway. Someone's got to put the Holden name up in lights."

Jess chuckled. "Yeah, and Montana is doing a great job of that with her barrel racing." He couldn't help teasing his little brother about Montana's win over the weekend. Colt had been winning too, but he'd taken a third place win that weekend. Both of them were trying to pick up enough points to qualify for the National Finals Rodeo championships in Las Vegas in November. They needed every point they could earn. That meant long hours, hard driving and dedication. Colt had been going strong and was rising to the top of the leader board. Montana had started the race late but was doing great. But time was running out. Pressure was on both of them.

Because of this, Jess had chosen not to mention the problem with the cattle to Colt until after he knew something concrete. He'd decided to tell Luke and Montana after they got home—which would be sometime the next morning. He'd hoped by then they'd know more about the situation.

"What's next for you?" he asked Colt, focusing on his little brother rather than the cattle.

"I'm heading down from Calgary but going to make several rodeos on the way in before hitting the Mule Hollow rodeo. My head's spinning and the tires on my trailer are smoking from the pace. But I'm doin' okay. I talked to Mom and she's planning on coming to see me ride in Mule Hollow."

"That's good," Jess said, but feeling nothing. Colt was the baby and had bought in early to their mother's excuses for leaving them behind. Not interested in talking about her, Jess's thoughts went to his long day. Church had pretty much been a disaster and he'd been beating himself up over it all afternoon as he drove around in the pastures observing cattle.

Gabi had seemed different at church. She'd been stiff and almost non-talkative. When the service was over, she'd disappeared quickly. He wasn't sure what the problem was, but he got the feeling it was him. Of course she'd caught him staring at least twice and he'd gotten the impression that she wasn't happy about that in the least.

That made two of them. What was he thinking, chasing after the vet tech?

"You there, Jess?"

Colt's question pulled Jess back to the conversation. "Yeah, I'm here. I just have a lot on my mind."

"You're okay with seeing Mom?"

His brothers knew he was less welcoming than they were, but they didn't judge him for it. Each of them dealt with their childhood in their own way. "I'll be here to watch you ride, Colt, and I'll be…" He paused. How *would* he be? Try as he might there was no way he could forgive his mother or welcome her as if she'd been a regular loving mother.

"She hates what she did, Jess." Colt's soft words echoed over the static-filled line. "She wishes she could take it back and do the right thing by us back then."

The words grated. "Yeah, so do I." Travis Tritt's famous "Here's a Quarter, Call Someone Who Cares" played through Jess's mind.

As far as he was concerned, it was a little too late. Way late.

* * *

The veterinarian's office was always swamped on Monday mornings. Today was no different. The place was alive with the ringing of telephone lines and the barking of dogs and puppies. Seeing patients every second kept Susan working through the morning. Tending to phones, helping with shots, weight and temperature, and everything else that came with the territory of vet assistant, kept Gabi equally busy.

It was almost eleven before they got their first breather.

"If this keeps up, I'll have to hire an office manager to relieve you," Susan said.

Inputting client information into the computer, Gabi's fingers flew across the keys as fast as she could move them. "I'll vote yes on that. My tongue is hanging out."

Susan chuckled. "Mine too. But I'm so blessed. My daddy taught me that a busy life is a blessing. Can be tiring sometimes, but a blessing."

"I can tell you, you and me are two really, *really* blessed people, if this morning is any indication."

"Business is good and I'm not complaining. Now, while we have a minute…" Susan said, settling against the office counter "…the Matchmaking Posse was all over Jess showing up and sitting with you at church."

"Ha! He sat with me because Applegate seated us together."

Susan grinned at that. "Shame on him."

"I don't want them getting all geared up for a romance, Susan."

"That might be hard to stop. There was no doubt in their minds that he came to church for one reason and one reason only. That was to see you. Even if it weren't true, that's what they read into it. I'm thinking they aren't wrong, Gabi. What's been going on out there on the ranch while you were looking for these plants? Come on, girl-talk time."

Gabi sighed. "What's not to be attracted to? The man is gorgeous."

"Then what's the problem?"

"I'm not ready to date again. On top of that, I don't want some cowboy who comes to church for me and not for God."

"Oh, yeah, I can see how that is a terrible, terrible thing."

Gabi didn't miss the teasing in Susan's words. "Later, when I do start dating, I'm going to be looking for a guy who puts God first. I picked poorly last time." She'd told Susan about Phillip and how he'd run as fast as he could the minute she'd found the Lord.

She didn't go into her drinking history but continued to keep it private.

"That's rough. I get where you're coming from now," Susan said.

"God is the most important thing in my life. He is number one. A guy who spruces up and comes to church to be near me is a total turn off to me. My next guy has to love God first and then me. Nothing else will do."

Susan's eyebrows lifted momentarily. "Strong words."

Gabi took a deep breath. "Yeah, I know, they sound harsh, don't they?"

"Very. But given your background I can understand where you're coming from. I have a friend over in Ranger who married a guy who told her God was the most important aspect of their lives. Told her what she wanted to hear, but once they were married he began pulling her away from church and her family. It ended badly. I guess if I was in your shoes, losing a fiancé like you did over your salvation, I'd be extra cautious, too."

Gabi gave her a regretful look. "I'm not settling for anything less. Jess Holden is a good-looking guy. There is something about him that I can't deny being attracted to. But I'm a strong woman. I am." She tapped her heart to emphasize where she'd grown strong since loving

God. God's strength was helping her overcome her past. "And I will not let myself get tangled up in a situation that's going to pull me away from my main goal right now, drawing closer to God and trying to do His will in my life."

"Boy, that's a tough one. The matchmakers will have to understand that. Are you going to be okay going out to Jess's this afternoon?" Susan looked apologetic that she'd have to send Gabi where she might not want to go.

"Oh, sure I am. I *want* to help him find whatever is wrong with his cattle. That's why I've spent so much time going over the possible plants that could be causing this. I want to help."

Susan smiled. "You are just too good to be true. I'm sure glad you came along when you did."

The praise touched Gabi. "Thanks, I'm so glad to earn my keep." And that was the truth. She really liked Susan and the clinic, and was feeling more content than she ever had in her life. "Are you sure you're not going to need me this afternoon?"

"I've implanted a ton of embryos by myself before I had the luxury of an assistant so I'll do okay today." Susan pushed away from the counter and headed toward the back. "You go on out there when you're ready. Tell Jess we should have the blood smear back soon so we'll know if we're looking at anything infectious that could spread to the entire herd and Luke's rodeo stock."

"I'll tell him."

"And good luck on staying out of trouble." Susan paused holding the door. "Who knows, Jess coming to church for you could lead to figuring out why he doesn't come in the first place. I've always been curious about that. Luke is faithful, and a hard worker at all the church functions. I can't help wondering why Jess is so much the opposite."

The phone rang before Gabi had time to comment on that. "Mule Hollow Veterinary Clinic," she said, picking up the line.

"Gabi, hey, this is Jess."

Of course it would be the object of their discussion—and of course her pulse did a silly jump, skip and a backflip at the sound of his voice. "Hey, Jess," she answered, not at all thrilled with the sound of her own voice squeaking. "What's up?"

"I've got a situation out here," he drawled, his tone grave. "I just found two more dead heifers."

They were dead all right. Gabi had made some quick calls to cancel afternoon appointments and moved them to different timeslots for Susan. Afterwards they'd headed straight out to Jess's place. As they'd hoped, the time of death had been within bounds of necropsy. Sad to say that a dead animal was a break in the case for them, but it was true. This was exactly what they needed to help solve this problem.

Putting everything else about Jess out of mind, Gabi was excited about the possibility of figuring this out. He'd come to church to see her, but she couldn't help wonder—or even hope—that maybe, just maybe he'd come to seek God's help in dealing with his cattle situation. Maybe he'd decided that he'd been away too long and showing God a little love would be a good thing.

Who knew? But a necropsy was in order and could take that worried crinkle out of the corners of his eyes.

If they found answers.

Susan made quick order out of the necropsy. The contents of the heifers' stomachs didn't disclose what the animals had eaten, but she took samples of everything to send off to the lab. The liver did show damage and that was enough to make them continue looking for a plant that could poison and harm the liver.

A worried shadow in his eyes, Jess watched while they performed the necropsy.

"So do you think we're going to get any answers?" he asked after a few minutes. "I called Luke and told him. He and Montana will be in late tonight. He was worried, like I knew he would be. I'd sure like to have something for him when he gets in other than more dead cattle."

Susan assured him they would have something in a few days. "With no rain and these drought conditions, you and all the other ranchers are facing the problem of your ratios. Most of these plants we're talking about are eaten but in a ration with nutritional plants that keep the ratio in balance."

"We're already feeding hay," Jess said, in defense, looking as if Susan had hauled off and slapped him. It was priceless. Gabi thought it was kind of cute, him thinking she was stepping all over his pride.

"I see that," Susan said, not taking offense herself. "But something is up somewhere, Jess."

"I get that," he agreed, his frustration plain on his face.

Gabi felt bad for him and filled with determination to help. She would do everything she could to figure this out.

After Susan had finished, she left Gabi behind to continue finding plant samples. Since she'd ridden out with Susan, Jess had assured her that he would take Gabi home after they searched for the killer plant.

"Let's do this thing," Gabi said, hands on her hips, she gave him a nod. "We may have to wait for test results to come back, but Susan narrowed our search to plants that damage the liver. So let's get crackin'."

Though he was intensely concerned by the dead cattle, her comment caused his lips to lift into a smile. "That's the best news I've heard all day."

Knowing she'd helped brighten his day boosted her spirits. With a little too much spring in her step, she headed toward the back of his truck. "I printed a color photo of each plant that we need to watch for." She laid them out, really enjoying the fact that she had the opportunity to make this cowboy's day. At the moment she didn't concentrate on the fact that she liked that bit of power. When the man smiled at her, her insides quivered with excitement. "By the time the results come back we may already have this mystery solved. Are you with me on that?" She held up her hand for a high-five of agreement.

Jess's eyes brightened and he lifted his hand and lightly slapped hers. "I'm with you. Just lead the way."

Chapter Seven

Jess had been feeling pretty low. With cattle dying in twos and threes, it was understandable. But with Susan's expertise and Gabi's positive attitude, he was feeling more optimistic.

They'd started the search in the pasture surrounding where they found the last dead cattle. The heifer had died in an area that had a large wooded and brush-filled gulley cutting through it. There were cattle grazing all across the pasture and some could be seen coming from the brush.

"I want to start there," she said, pointing toward the gulley. "That looks interesting, don't you think?"

"I'm willing to give anything a shot," he said, and meant it.

"Then let's hit it. You know the routine." She pulled out her plastic baggies and her little book, waggling her eyebrows at him as she stuffed it and the baggies into a small flat backpack that she slid her arms through. She exuded confidence and a good humor that couldn't help but boost his spirits as they headed into the woods.

"I feel like a detective right now," she said. "All I need is a trench coat and a fedora and I'd be set. What do you think?" She gave him an over-the-shoulder grin and then rattled off several old television detectives.

Jess laughed. One thing he was absolutely certain of—Gabi might feel like a detective but she didn't look anything like one.

"What's that laugh for, mister?" She smiled and showed him her dimple.

He stumbled over a dip in the trail and *almost* took a nose-dive at her feet.

"Now, that's grace in motion," she quipped, stopping to stare at a plant. Jess was staring at her, and could not help it…he had cattle dying, but at the moment he had to admit that he was having a great time.

Gabi felt a little self conscious at the way Jess was staring at her. She had on her boots which enabled her to stomp through the underbrush where needed, but she'd chosen to follow one of the many cow trails. It wound beneath the trees, dappled sunlight filtered through the mesquite and oak trees sprinkled about, highlighting tangled masses of berry vines covering the ground and yaupon bushes. This area of Texas was the best of both worlds to Gabi. Sitting on the edge of hill country, it was combination of hill country rock and mesquite mixed with oak trees and grass. The grass, though, was quickly disappearing with the lack of a good slow rain. This was not a thick, dark woods, but rather, it had areas where the sun filtered in heavily and plants thrived. Other areas it was shadowed and the air was thick with heat and the scents of earth.

Gabi wasn't thinking much about any of this though as she led the way through the woods. She chattered about random things to tease smiles out of her handsome cohort. She smiled to herself, understanding fully that the man was going to think she was absolutely senseless. That was all right. She hadn't liked seeing him worried. But she knew she was tenacious and wouldn't stop until she found out what was killing his cattle.

She also wouldn't stop until she had Jess all figured out. The man interested her on so many levels. No, it wasn't just that he made her pulse do things that might have sent an older person to the E.R. And it wasn't that she liked seeing the gleam of surprise in his eyes as much as she just plain liked his eyes. It was much more—things she couldn't put her finger on and things she could. She liked how hard he seemed to work. And how much he seemed to care about this place and his brothers, whom he was trying so hard to protect from the fact that their ranch was in a jam. She didn't know what kind of a boyfriend he would be—which was of no interest to her, she reminded herself strongly. But she liked who he was otherwise. The man was a stand-up guy. And that was just plain attractive.

Not that she was attracted to him…

Okay, so she was attracted but not acting on that attraction. She was only trying to lift the guy's spirits with her teasing conversations.

She couldn't help it if he seemed to like it.

As they tramped around talking and searching, they found a few poisonous plants that weren't usually much of a threat but Gabi took samples anyway. They didn't cause liver damage either, so she doubted they were going to be a problem, but she wanted to document them.

"So you used to get into trouble and make your grandmother worry?"

His question came out of nowhere, taking her by surprise.

They'd been searching for about three hours,

chatting and goofing off. Though she'd messed up early in life and mentioned that she'd made her Gram worry, she hadn't expected any response. Jess was following her off the trail when he had asked the question.

"And my mother," she added, as she scrambled to figure out what to say about her past. "Not my proudest accomplishment. I'm sure you understand that." She shot him a smile and hoped to turn the conversation to him and away from her. "Isn't that more of a guy thing, to give his parents a hard time?"

She crouched down to look at a plant growing close to the ground as she continued to talk away, nervous about things getting too personal. "I'm sure you probably had your moments. I'm not making excuses for myself, but I guess making parents worry is part of growing up and finding our own way. It can't be avoided to some extent. Don't you agree?" She was just rattling away, and Jess hadn't commented.

"I *guess* so," he finally said, his voice casual, his expression flat.

She'd looked up from poking around at the little plant and caught the funny expression on his face. "I guess so?" she repeated. "Wait a minute. Are you telling me you never messed up and made your parents worry about you?" Ha! She knew better than that. She hadn't known him long but she knew that Jess had probably been a typical mischievous little boy and more than likely a wild teenager. "There is no way you didn't cause your parents to turn gray headed early worrying about you growing up. No way at all."

A look of detachment descended on his face. "I *never* made my parents worry."

"Get out of here. No way!" The man was teasing her. She stood, grinning at him. "You are pulling my leg. Not that you don't seem to have your act together now, but I know you pushed a few buttons."

He shrugged and looked…embarrassed. "Gabi, you can only push buttons if someone cares."

It was her turn to look embarrassed as it hit her—he'd told her that he and his brothers didn't have the best childhood. What had she been thinking?

"I—I hadn't thought about it in those terms. I'm…" She stumbled over her words. It wasn't often that she was at a loss for them. How could she have been so careless?

Reaching out, he tugged her ponytail. "It's all right," he assured her, giving a teasing grin intended to make her feel better—it just made it worse. "I got over it a long time ago."

That was an odd thing to say. *Change the*

subject, Gabi. Change the subject. She'd never been really diplomatic, and just because she'd become a Christian hadn't changed that. She was praying about that too, among tons of other stuff. God had His hands full where she was concerned.

"I should keep my mouth shut and let the awkward moment pass," she said. "But I can't. Instead I'm going to stick my foot into my mouth even deeper and ask why your parents didn't care. That just sounds awful. Sorry, but it does."

A ray of sunlight shifted onto his face, as if God was putting His hand on Jess to comfort him and she suddenly wanted with all of her heart to do the same thing.

She wondered if Jess had any clue that he looked like a lost little boy in that moment. Everyone cared whether their parents cared or not. Even adult men.

He looked as if he was going to clam up. But, thinking, he pulled a leaf from an oak limb dangling near his head. For a moment he studied the leaf like it was the most interesting leaf God had ever created. "It's no big secret," he said at last. "Everyone knows my father only cared about his alcohol. He lived for that bottle and nothing else. And my mother, she got tired of it—*all* of it, including us, and she skipped out when we were little. I was ten, Luke fourteen and Colt eight."

His dad had been an alcoholic.

Gabi almost flinched at the news. The way Jess'd relayed the info told her instantly how devastating and hard that had been on him. Her mouth went dry, thinking of her own situation which was way too fresh on her mind. "I'm sorry," she managed to say, blood rushing in her ears. Jess Holden was a strong, adult male and the clarity of his father's actions was etched deeply into him. Cut deep and raw like an open wound. Never, never would she have wanted to do that to her family. And yet she'd very easily been on the path.

"No biggie," he said, as if he didn't care when clearly he did. "Like I said, that was a long time ago."

Gabi needed to look somewhere else, at a plant, at a tree, at a gopher hole. Anywhere, but into this cowboy's pain-filled eyes.

And anger. There was anger in those eyes and that cut right to Gabi's core.

This could have been me. This could have been her own adult child hating her one day if she hadn't awakened to the path she'd almost chosen for her life.

Her knees buckled as the heat and the reality all seemed to hit her at once. "I need to sit down," she whispered.

"Are you all right?" Jess was beside her instantly, his hand on her elbow as she took a weak step toward a large, flat rock.

"You look about as white as milkweed juice. And you're clammy, too."

"I'm fine. I—I just need to sit down for a minute."

He held her arm as she sank to the rock. Placing her elbows on her knees, she thrust her fingers in her hair and stared at the ground between her feet.

"This heat can sneak up on you out here." Jess patted her back, comforting her. Gabi gave a hollow laugh, lifting her head just a little as she nodded. What else could she do?

She certainly wasn't going to tell the man she was…that she'd had her own issues with alcohol. Nope, no way in the world she was doing that. Her life had been a mess that would rival those sleazy reality television shows out there. She cringed and broke out into a cold sweat all over again. Her and Phillip's life had been a real mess.

What would Jess think of her? Her hands knotted into fists and she dug deep to pull herself from the hole she'd just fallen into.

Taking the bottle of water he had pulled out

of the backpack, Gabi took a big swallow and then forced herself to look at him. "Give me a minute and I'll be fine." She held up the water bottle. "I should have been drinking more of this."

"I should have been making sure that you did—"

"It wasn't your fault, Jess. I'm my own keeper, you know. I'm my own keeper," she said again then repeated the words in her head for a third time like a chant. Jess's dad had been an alcoholic— "Look, sorry I snapped. Really, thanks for looking out for me." She felt horrible. "And I'm real sorry about your dad."

He shrugged. "Kids deal with that sort of stuff all the time. Sadly, me and my brothers weren't the first and we won't be the last. I'm not going to let it ruin my life today. Kids grow up and take control of their lives. They get to make their own choices."

"True," Gabi said, her hand trembled as she took another swig of water and tried to meet his gaze.

"And I can promise you," he said, his words harsh. "Dealing with an alcoholic isn't something I'll ever have to deal with again. Ever."

Chapter Eight

Jess dropped off Gabi at her house not long after she'd overheated. He'd felt bad about that, and though they'd both been hot, sweaty and ready to get cleaned up, he'd offered to buy her dinner at Sam's. She'd declined the offer though, opting instead to go on home to cool off.

It was probably for the best, he thought, watching her stroll through the picket fence and close the little gate.

"You sure you're all right?" he called, not able to put his finger on it, but sensing something wasn't right. Maybe it was him, after all he was the one who'd opened his big mouth and told her his life story.

He *never* did that. And here he'd gone and dredged up his past—oh, he'd sidestepped like crazy once he'd realized what he'd done but it was too late. Gabi was already throwing pity his way.

"I'm fine," she called from the door. "You pumped enough water down me to drown a horse. Talk to you tomorrow." She slipped inside and he watched the door close behind her.

Intending on going home, he backed out of the drive but he didn't make it far, deciding at the last minute to swing by Sam's. Pulling his truck into a spot in front of the diner, he headed inside. The sign beside the door declared "eat at your own peril" but everyone knew that Sam's cooking was home cooking. No peril involved. Unless you chose his meat loaf—all bets were off on that hunk of burning fire. Sam concocted it to set a cowboy's mouth on fire. And it caught its fair share of unsuspecting greenhorns off guard. While making a room full of onlookers hoot with laughter.

It was a slow crowd when he entered. And though he was a little this side of fresh, he didn't let it stop him, Sam's was made for the working cowboy. Dust covered and sweaty was Sam's best customer. His kind had kept the diner open through the years in between the oil bust that had sent a major portion of Mule Hollow's population packing, and the Mule Hollow matchmakers' "wives wanted" campaign. Crazy but successful, those advertisements for would-be wives for the lonesome cowboys of the town had been a success. But in between the two epic events, it had been the hard-working, sometimes crusty, cowboy that had kept this little town alive.

The town had been different then, a sad assortment of terribly weathered clapboard buildings that, with so many businesses going belly-up after the oil bust, resembled a ghost town. Now, after Lacy Matlock and the ladies had painted it every color under the sun— and he meant that literally—it looked bright and shiny and different. He, like every other cowboy in the room, wasn't going to say he liked the two-story bright pink hair salon that could be seen all the way at the crossroads. Or the bright blue building with yellow trim that was now Pete's Feed and Seed…or the purple or lime green or any of the other outlandish colors that each building was painted. But it had changed the face of the town and people were here.

Smiling, happy people. And they just kept coming. That was nice. There was an energy to Mule Hollow that was undeniable and all the cowboys welcomed it. But still, it was nice that Sam's had remained true to the working cowboys.

Feeling at loose ends, deep in thought, Jess

moved through the diner to grab a cowhide-covered stool at the counter. There was something to be said about familiarity—it was comforting. Jess felt better just being here. As a kid they'd never had much money to splurge on a breakfast or lunch on their own. But, after Luke went to work for Mr. Matlock, Luke'd bring them all in some days after Mr. Matlock had paid him extra for being a good hand. He always told Luke it was a bonus—they looked back at it now and knew that Mac Matlock was looking out for them. As did Sam. He always made sure they had extra helpings when they came in and there would always be something extra from the kitchen that he'd pawn off on them to take home. Of course when they'd come to Mule Hollow, their mother had already skipped out on them and they were craving something that was remotely like a home-cooked meal.

This was a good place.

"Hey, Sam," he said as he propped his elbows on the polished counter.

"How's it goin', Jess? You find anything out about them cattle of yors that come up dead?"

"Not yet."

"I heard Susan sent Gabi out thar to yor place to check plants."

"Yes, sir. She spent the afternoon searching

and is supposed to come out again tomorrow." He'd watch her closer tomorrow and make sure she drank more water.

Sam nodded. "That's good. You two gett'n along okay? She was purdy mad at you the other day."

"I think we are. That was all a misunderstanding. I told her I wasn't in here bragging about rescuing her. I wouldn't do that."

"I know that. She jest got a little touchy, what with us all jumping her about that stunt she pulled and all."

Jess didn't add to that comment. He'd already said his piece about it that day. Thing was, the woman was bright. He could tell it today by the way she took hold of the toxic plant issue. She'd just made what he deemed a bad judgment call the day of the flash flood. "I'm glad it turned out good and I was able to help." He grinned. "I like her. She's one smart cookie."

"Yup. My Adela is happier than a peach that she's come back here to live. And that makes me happy. She had a little trouble but is doing good now. What can I get fer you tonight? The rush is about to happen so you got here jest in the nick of time."

Jess laughed, ordered his meal. He wondered what kind of trouble Gabi had had? *None of your business, Holden.*

Maybe so, but that didn't stop him from thinking about it.

Something had happened today, he just didn't know what it was. She'd gotten overheated for a minute but then, despite his protest, she'd brushed it off and gotten back to work. There was a lot he wanted to ask Gabi but when his steak came, he ate it without asking one question about her...kept his mouth full and his questions to himself.

When he was done eating he headed back out to his truck. He glanced down toward Gabi's. What was she was doing? Did she feel better? Crazy as it was, he wondered if she might want to go catch a late movie in Ranger?

What was wrong with him?

He had cattle dropping dead in the pasture and he was thinking about snagging a date with Gabi Newberry!

If he didn't know better, he'd think it had been him who'd gotten too much sun today.

"Hey, hey, Mr. Holden," Gabi said, the next morning as she pulled up next to the barn. "You ready to go find our toxic plant?" Thankfully she felt better today. She'd let herself get in the dumps the night before, after hearing about Jess's past. His dad especially. Alcohol scared her as much as it made Jess angry. She had decided that today there would be no digging into his past or hers.

"Let's do it," he said, opening the passenger door of his truck. "I'm happy to say I didn't find any more dead cattle this morning."

"Praise the Lord," she said, hopping from her truck, her small backpack dangling from her hand, she headed to where he stood holding open the door for her. He had on well-worn jeans, and a black T-shirt that stretched across his broad chest. She ignored the way her pulse tripped over itself when he grinned and showed a tiny dimple she hadn't noticed before.

"I'm telling you, I feel lucky today, Jess."

He laughed and a teasing glint sparkled in his eyes. "That's what I like to hear."

Butterflies tickled her insides, which she ignored. "Then stick with me, buddy. I've got that covered b'cause I'm feeling God's kinda luck today and that's a good, good thing." She'd reminded herself of that last night when she'd gotten down. Every day was a blessing and she was here to enjoy it.

Today was a new day.

Her past was her past. She was never going back to that lifestyle. Jess had made a promise to himself never to have to deal with an alcoholic again. She'd made herself a similar promise, never to drink again, and with God's help she was going to keep that promise forever.

One arm crooked over the open window, the other on the steering wheel, Jess headed back toward the crop of trees they'd begun investigating the day before. Zack Brown was singing a peppy tune on the radio, and though he had a problem with his cattle that could be potentially devastating to the ranch's bottom line, he felt great. He cocked his head and let his gaze slide over Gabi. Her ponytail hung across her shoulder and she was scanning the pasture. He noticed her slightly upturned nose, and her lips quirking upward, as if she was always ready to smile.

Something he wasn't familiar with stirred inside his chest. He whistled along with the radio.

"I'm not the only one in a good mood this morning."

"I feel good about this, Gabi." He tightened his grip on the steering wheel, unable to explain the way he'd felt when she'd driven up earlier. Instead he didn't analyze it as he nodded toward the gray-blue morning sky. "Look at that sky. Rain is in the forecast."

She studied the dark clouds in the distance. "I'm all for it but," she chuckled, her eyes shifting mischievously at him. "I just hope if it happens this time, it will be a little slower rain than the last time."

"Hey, don't worry 'bout it," he said. "I'll take better care of you today."

She clasped a hand to her heart. "I am *so* thankful."

"There you go again, hurting my feelings."

"Ha! I've only known you for a little while, Jess, but something tells me you do not wear your feelings on your sleeve."

That was an understatement. Some things learned early in life lasted. "Yeah, there you're right." Their eyes met and he felt like there was an undercurrent of understanding passing between them. He didn't normally talk to others about his past but for some reason he'd talked to Gabi. "So just holler when you see a place you want to investigate." Needing suddenly to steer the conversation away from where it had gone, he started scanning the pasture. He focused on what the cattle were eating as they passed.

"Let's start in the same area they were in the day before. I want to follow another cow path heading off in a different direction from the one we already tracked."

"Sounds good." He drove to the spot. He carried the backpack and let Gabi take the lead.

She had her hair up in her usual ponytail and her uniform of tank top and jeans.

"So how many plants do we have so far?" he asked after they'd been tramping around for about an hour. Despite his tries he could not rid himself of his growing curiosity about the ball of fire that was leading him through his gulley for the second day in a row.

She was quieter today—even though she still bantered with him, she was more subdued. "Seven counting the ones we found yesterday."

Jess scratched his temple in consternation. "That's unbelievable—it's a wonder I have any live cattle at all."

"This isn't uncommon though—" Suddenly her ponytail snagged on a thorny bush. "Ow!" she exclaimed as it jerked tight. Firmly caught, she angled her head attempting to free herself.

"Wait," Jess demanded, hurrying to help. If she tried to jerk free, the bush would retaliate, slapping at her across the neck and most likely leaving a nasty scratch. They were only a couple inches apart and he had to pull strand by strand from the grasp of the thorny bush.

The sweet scent of her hair tickled his nose as he worked. His fingers felt big and clumsy when she twisted her head slightly to get a look at him.

"Just let me yank it," she said.

"No. Hold still," he urged, concentrating on getting her loose without letting the sharp inch-long spikes injure her—or him—in the process.

She groaned. "Am I attached for life?" she asked, her gaze dropping to his lips and then jumping back up to his eyes. He suddenly couldn't think straight and his pulse was doing something weird that had him feeling weak in the knees.

When her clear green eyes darkened as if she felt the same thing, his heart did a cannonball dive straight to his boots. Jerking unexpectedly at the emotion he impaled his finger on a long hard thorn.

"Ow!" he exclaimed, staring at the thorn stuck in his index finger.

Gabi jumped at his yelp and her hair came free from the thorns. Immediately she grabbed his hand. "Let me see," she said.

He thought she was breathless too and his pulse beat erratically at her touch. He swallowed hard, his glance skimming the blood running down his hand. He focused on her instead, even as perspiration pricked his forehead and things about him shifted.

"You're bleeding bad," Gabi gasped, looking up at him. "And you're *green!* Leapin' lizards—you need to sit down!"

Yes, he did. Spots blinked in front of him and

his head spun. Gabi dragged him to a fallen tree, pushed him to sit down.

"You faint at the sight of blood!" she accused bending down to stare at him. Her eyes widened in dismay at the discovery of the truth— "Oh, no, you don't," she exclaimed looking into his eyes. With that said, she grabbed him by the neck and shoved his head between his knees.

"But how is that?" she asked, her voice coming at him through a tunnel. Dismay erupting from her. "You watched us open up that dead cow yesterday? Nothing could be as gross as that."

Jess focused on the dirt and grass between his boots and prayed he didn't fall down at Gabi's boot tips. "It's only my own blood that bothers me."

"Just breathe deeply then, and hold on. This may hurt but we need to get the blood stopped and clean you up." She dabbed at his finger, then with expert firmness pulled the thorn free. Totally in control—good thing someone was—she held pressure on the puncture. All he could do was stay down, study her boots and wait for his stomach to stop swaying and his head to stop spinning.

"Getting rid of the thorn and blood is going to help, right?"

"Yes, in a minute." Sucking in air, he felt less

woozy finally. Sitting up he hiked a shoulder, looking pretty much like a loser. He met her wide eyes.

She gave him a hesitant smile, her eyes crinkling around the edges. He saw her lip twitch and then, unable to hold it in, she laughed. It bubbled out small then as her hoots echoed through the woods and despite feeling like a loser, he laughed too.

"You are a rough-and-tough cowboy," she said after an instant. "And you were as weak as a kitten just a few minutes ago."

"Yeah, well, I don't do well on boats, either."

Her grin was like sunshine. "I love it. I'm sorry, but every hero needs a weakness."

"Gee, thanks for your sympathy," he teased, trying to remain in the moment and not to return to the dangerous slippery slope he was wobbling on when this happened. Staring into her twinkling eyes was not helping.

One minute she was staring at him with eyes that drew him like a bee to sugar water. Oh, yeah, he was thinking about kissing her—but panic flickered in her eyes, her gaze shifting as if taking flight and then she did.

"Look at that!" she exclaimed suddenly, moving to kneel beside a hoofprint.

So much for that.

"If you're feeling all right, we need to follow this cow."

Feeling all right? His head was spinning and it had nothing to do with the sight of his own blood.

And his ego was in the Dumpster.

Feeling all right?

Sure. Great.

Not that she gave him enough time to tell one way or the other before she was up and traipsing off in a new direction following some semi-hidden hoofprints mixed in the dirt and underbrush.

He stood there watching her go. What had he been thinking anyway? He'd gotten all woozy looking at his blood—not exactly the best way to impress a girl.

Nope. The woman was out there racing through the woods laughing her head off...

Way to go, cowboy.

Chapter Nine

"Sampson checks out great," Susan said to Esther Mae on Wednesday as she led the spunky redhead from the examination room. Esther had brought in her small dog for its shots. The ball of black fur weighed about four pounds and had bright, black eyes that looked out from beneath a shaggy mane of hair that fell over his eyes. A Dorkie, the tiny dog was a cross between a dachshund and a Yorkshire terrier.

"Come here, cutie," Gabi said, taking the wiggling fur ball from Susan. He immediately jumped in her arms and tried to lick her cheeks. "Oh, Esther Mae, he's great!"

"I know, he's been a blessing. The little cutie patootie has won mine and Hank's hearts. But he is extremely mischievous. You have to watch out for him all the time."

Susan and Gabi both burst into laughter. Norma Sue, who had come with Esther Mae and remained in the waiting room, hooted.

"Like his owner," Gabi was the first to say, clearly understanding that she'd been double-timed today. Norma Sue had used the time she was in the waiting room probing for info on what was going on between her and Jess. Nothing, Gabi had tried to convince her. But it wasn't working. The matchmakers were going to believe what they wanted to believe. And they believed that there was more between her and Jess.

They had no clue that there couldn't be. Not that she was looking but she knew with their past…not so much.

"Well," Esther Mae said, with an impish look. "Life would be a real stick in the mud if we all acted perfect, wouldn't it?"

"That's the truth," Norma Sue huffed. "Especially where you're concerned."

"Where *both* of you are concerned," Susan teased, just as the door opened and her husband strode inside.

"Hello, ladies," Cole Turner said. Sweeping his straw Stetson from his head, he strode straight over to Susan, draped his arms around her and gave her one good kiss. "And how's my favorite vet doing?"

Susan blushed, gave him a second quick kiss and smiled. "She's doing wonderful now."

They were a striking couple. Susan was tall, blond and willowy, about five feet ten or so, and Cole dark headed and standing at least six foot three. They just fit together.

"I was heading home early and thought I'd check to see if you could get away for a midweek date with your favorite contractor."

"Oh, sounds wonderful." Susan, eyes bright, turned to Gabi who was at the reception desk. "How's my schedule look this afternoon?"

Gabi glanced down at the screen, though she already knew that Esther Mae was the last client for the day. "It says for you to skip out an hour early while you can, before some emergency brings you back here. Go. I'll take calls for the night and only bother you if something major comes up that I can't handle."

Cole gave her an appreciative wink. "Did I tell you that I love you?" He laughed.

"Every week since I've been here."

"Well, I mean it. Thanks for helping me get some quality time with my wife."

"You're welcome." Gabi felt all happy inside as she and the two matchmakers watched Susan and Cole leave hand in hand.

"I just love seeing that," Esther Mae cooed. "New love is a beautiful thing."

"Yes, it is, don't you think, Gabi?" Norma Sue pumped.

Knowing exactly what they were up to, Gabi rubbed noses with Sampson. "Yes I do. That's why I'm in love with this little guy."

"How about that handsome hunk of a Holden man?" Esther Mae scooted closer to the counter and looked at Gabi expectantly. As if Gabi was going to spill the beans about what had been happening out in those woods with her? Ha!

Hardly.

"Esther Mae, just like I told Norma Sue, don't even go there. Y'all know why I'm here and it doesn't have anything to do with finding a man." She had no problem keeping her mouth shut about this. If they got wind of her attraction, there was no stopping them.

"Hey, *we're* the matchmakers," Esther Mae said, proving Gabi's point. "And we haven't had to do anything to put you two together. Seems to me God's been doing a pretty good job of that all on His own."

Norma Sue was just staring at Esther Mae and then she looked at Gabi and nodded her head. "She does have a point there."

While the two continued their conversation about her life, Gabi kept her thoughts to herself. To be quite frank, she was going to miss going to Jess's place every day. But it was for the best. She was pretty positive they would discover Jess's problem soon and then there would be no need for her to go out there any longer. She had enjoyed her time roaming Jess's property for the last few days, and of course there was the fact that the man made her feel like she'd just stepped out of an airplane without a parachute.

Hello—the man was gorgeous, funny, and he practically fainted at the sight of his own blood! Cute. And Gabi knew she would come to Jess's rescue any day of the week.

For a gal who wasn't planning on getting involved with someone, she sure was having a hard time remembering that. All the more reason for this to be done soon. She was here to work on herself. And no one but her and God knew just how much work she needed. Even her Gram didn't know the whole truth.

She didn't trust herself in so many ways....

Especially when she let herself dwell on what Jess had been through as a kid. Try as she might, she couldn't stop thinking about that. His dad had been an alcoholic. The word vibrated in her head like a migraine.

Staring into his Jess's eyes the day before, it had hit her—an image of the expression on his face when he found out she'd had her own battle with drinking. Her stomach soured with embarrassment just thinking about what he or anyone would think if they knew.

Nope, anything between them was strictly business, because anything else—anything personal—was doomed.

And she had no one to blame but herself.

"Toxic plants," Applegate grunted. App was sitting at his usual table at the front of the diner, deep into a game of checkers with Stanley. "Ain't that a kick in the pants," his words bounced off the walls of the packed diner.

"Shor is," Stanley agreed, spitting sunflower husks like a machine gun. The shells hit the spittoon dead-on—and why not, the two old-timers had had plenty of practice. It wasn't uncommon to see the small boys in town practicing their sunflower spitting.

This morning though, Sam's was booming with business as several tables were full of cowboys getting their breakfast before heading out to work. Jess was on his way to Oklahoma to deliver a load of cattle for Clint Matlock and he and Luke had met for breakfast. He had to get back by day's end so he could deliver some rodeo stock for Luke to a small town almost to Houston the next day.

"Yes, that's what they suspect," Jess assured the older man.

"Got you one purdy gal helpin' ya look," App thundered.

"Yup, it's real nice of Gabi ta help you out like that," Sam said, plopping two plates of eggs and bacon on the table in front of Luke and Jess. "She's a peach."

"Yes, she is," Luke agreed. "We owe her. Susan, too. But if Gabi hadn't gone out there with Jess and searched, we'd have been several days behind and probably have more head die too."

"That's the truth. I bet Susan is glad she hired such good help," App boomed.

"And did we say purdy, too," Stanley added, hiking a bushy brow and grinning at Jess. "You noticed that, didn't ya, son?"

Luke grinned across the table at him as more than a few eyes turned his way. "Yeah, Jess. Did you notice how pretty she is?"

He shot Luke a scowl. He didn't need anyone egging on the older men. "I noticed," was all he said.

"Purdy, smart, sweet and a good girl too. Now that's a winnin' combination, if you ask me," Sam said. "Of course I'm kinda partial to the kid. My Adela is so happy Gabi moved back here that I jest have ta thank God ever' day fer His blessings."

Jess nodded. "Everything you've said about Gabi is true. I'm also pretty sure she has good teeth and has had all her shots, too."

Three sets of graying eyebrows dipped along with Luke's hiked set.

Jess held his hands up. "Hey, don't look at me like that," he huffed, feeling a little pushed in a corner and not liking it. "Y'all are the ones talking about her like she's the best horse in the lineup."

Luke chuckled, bit off a piece of crisp bacon and chewed. After realizing the cattle were safe, he'd been highly excited to know that Jess and Gabi had spent so much time together.

"She *is* the best filly in the lineup," Sam said, defensively. "And one day soon some smart cowboy's gonna come along and sweep that little gal right off her feet."

Jess downed a fork full of fried egg and made no comment. He did however flashback to him standing in the woods with her while she tended to his bleeding finger. She'd probably thought he was a wimp, but all he could remember was how much he'd wanted to kiss her. How great she'd smelled and how pretty her eyes were, looking into his.

"You judging that blackberry cobbler contest at the fair this weekend?" App asked Jess. He jumped one of Stanley's black checkers and smiled triumphantly.

"Don't be smilin' like that, ya old goat," Stanley warned as he studied the game. "Ah-ha!" he moved his piece from the edge and took out an unprotected king. "That's what not payin' attention'll get ya."

Jess wasn't sure if anyone was paying any attention but he answered anyway. "Yes, this dumb cowboy doesn't turn down berry cobbler and y'all know it."

Sam had gone to the kitchen for more food but paused beside his table. "I'm sick of hearing those women boasting about their cobbler. Ever' year it's the same thing. Norma Sue and Esther Mae kin jest get plumb ornery about it."

Jess laughed. "Yeah, but I get all I want. And y'all know I've never, ever met a berry I didn't like. I like blackberries, strawberries, blueberries—"

Sam grinned like it was his last hurrah. "How about *New*berrys?"

Luke shook his head. "You walked right into that one, little brother."

Jess gave up. "Yes, Sam. But come on, what's not to like? She's a nice girl. Y'all like her, too."

"Yup. But if you ain't noticed, we're old as dirt and already had our turn at love," App said, almost at a normal volume. "We're tryin' ta help you out. But sometimes I thank you young bucks are short some important wires or somethin'."

"That's fer dad-gum shor," Stanley grunted, grabbing more sunflower seeds from the half-empty five-pound bag. "We're tryin' ta do our Christian duty and set you on the right path."

"And you ain't cooperatin' too all fired well," Sam snapped, then strode to the table by the jukebox where he plopped the plates of food in front of the hungry bunch of startled cowhands.

The old dudes were a little touchy today!

Jess met Luke's watchful eyes over the brim of his steaming coffee. His brother was having too good of a time with this.

But Jess wasn't falling for the bait. His mouth was shut.

If these fellas knew how much Gabi was on his mind, there would be no hope for him. He'd been thinking about her nonstop for the last few days.

He'd had to fight himself not to make up excuses to go by the clinic. But he wasn't going. No matter how much he was tempted.

Nope. He might have gone weak in the knees from the sight of his own blood before, but he'd never gone weak in the knees for a woman.

It had him feeling like his saddle had slipped

and he was riding sideways. Gabi Newberry made him feel things he wasn't used to feeling, and he wasn't real sure what to do about it.

One thing he did know—keep his mouth shut around these three old codgers.

They'd get a guy in trouble and enjoy every minute of it.

Nope, where Gabi was concerned, he was going to proceed with caution.

Chapter Ten

"Smell that cotton candy," Gabi said, inhaling deeply as she and Gram walked toward the County Fair on Friday morning. "I could eat my weight in that."

"Yes, but then you wouldn't have room for the cobbler."

"True." Gabi sighed. She'd agreed to be a judge in the Best Berry Cobbler contest and she'd been a bit nervous about it. Women took their cobbler dishes seriously in these parts. But, hey, she loved cobbler.

Excitement bubbled all around the fairgrounds that were alive with activity. Kids of all ages, shapes and color swarmed here and there, their laughter mixed with the bellows and neighs of goats, halter heifers, commercial heifers and more.

As they were nearing the chicken pens,

shrieks and laughter broke out when chickens suddenly escaped and began flying everywhere.

Startled, Gabi and Adela paused as a little boy of about ten grabbed one chicken, tripped and fell face-first into a wet spot on the dirt floor.

Gabi started forward to help him, thinking he was going to be upset. But before she could get there, he popped up, grinned and raced after the escaped chicken.

"I guess that means he's okay," Gabi told Gram, smiling. "This is going to be fun," she added, excitement filling her. There was action everywhere.

"I was hoping you'd think so. Remember when you showed a pig and dressed him up in that little black tuxedo the night of the sale? You really seemed to love it back then."

Gabi remembered. "Homer was very handsome and went on to father a nation of little piglets with great genes." Somewhere along the way Gabi had started looking for more excitement than that found in the simple things in life. She'd picked a career that dealt with animals because she'd loved it. But somehow she'd gotten off track.

Adela's warm gaze drew Gabi and she knew Gram was thinking similar thoughts. "I think there could probably be some of his family competing here this week," she said, moving past the shared moment of understanding.

"I'd like to believe that." Gabi laughed. It wasn't unthinkable. Her hog had been a great one. Passing through the arena area they stopped here and there to speak to people they knew. About twenty minutes later they made it to the annex building where the art and food competition was being housed. The building was about fifty feet from the livestock barn, on a slight hill away from all the action. Rolled up garage doors were open on both sides so it was easy to see the buzz of activity going on down the hill.

Inside were tables set up with various cobblers already displayed. The aroma of the room was ripe with sweetness, and it had Gabi's stomach growling immediately.

"Yoo-hoo!" Esther Mae hustled up to them. Her cheeks were as pink as the shirt she wore—somewhere between fuchsia and plum. "Just in time. We're gearing up to get started. Rose Cantrell is heading up this competition but had to run down to the office for a minute and will be right back."

Then she saw Norma Sue and Jess from across the room. She hadn't seen him since Wednesday, and despite how it irritated her, wishing it wasn't so, she couldn't deny that she'd missed him.

His magnetizing gaze caught hers. She was certain that the sound of her heart banging in her chest could be heard by everyone.

There was nothing abnormal about this. Like this kind of feeling happened every day! But as he walked toward her, she knew this crazy connection between them was not like anything she'd ever felt. A week! She'd only known the cowboy for a week....

"I hear we're judging the berry cobbler contest together," he said, giving her that cute smile of his, the one that made him look as if he knew a secret that no one else knew.

"We are?" she managed to say, trying not to fall under the power of that smile. She glanced accusingly at Gram.

Adela, looking unbelievably innocent, smiled serenely.

Like a brick to her forehead, Gabi knew then and there that the conspiracy was on. Full steam ahead.

"I've got them!" Rose Cantrell called, hurrying into the building waving papers. "Sorry about the delay, but now that we have the score cards we can get started."

Not contrite at all about her deception, Adela introduced Gabi to Rose. Rose Cantrell owned a small, prickly pear jelly company and was married to the town deputy. Who had been a Texas Ranger and once protected Rose in the witness protection program. In less than two minutes, Gabi learned all about Rose's history as Ester Mae chattered away. Practically without taking a breath!

Rose blushed slightly. "Esther Mae, Gabi isn't here to learn about me." To Gabi she added, "Don't worry, there won't be a test later."

"Okay, but I'm ready if there is," Gabi teased, glad to have anything that would distract her from the man standing patiently beside her.

"Let's get this ball rolling," Norma Sue called from where she'd opened a closet door. "Y'all need to get in here while we get things ready."

"Excuse me?" Gabi said, certain she'd misunderstood. "In there?" Gabi crossed to Norma Sue and Jess followed.

"That's a new twist." Jess sounded as leery as she felt.

Rose looked apologetic. "The ladies decided on this part. Sorry it's so cramped. But it won't be for long."

Jess leaned over her shoulder and peered into the room, a weird expression on his face.

"Don't tell me," Gabi whispered, all too aware of him. "You're claustrophobic, too."

His tanned cheeks tinged a soft pink. "No."

"Sorry," she mumbled then bit her lip to hold back a chuckle.

"After we have a small bowl of each entry scooped up and numbered," Rose was explaining, "we'll call you out and you will sit at that table and begin your tasting." She pointed to a long table in the center of the room.

Gabi had spent hours searching pastures with Jess, feeling this attraction building over the week. And now, she and Jess were expected to step inside this closet and wait.

Just the two of them.

Suddenly Gabi wasn't laughing.

Looking into Jess's eyes, she knew that the joke was on her.

Apples. That was what Gabi's hair smelled like. It tickled his nose like the scent of a fresh-baked apple pie. He swallowed hard and tried to think about cobbler, not Gabi. But he'd had her on his mind for days.

And now, in a room the size of a saddlebag, it was hard to focus on anything *but* her.

Norma Sue grinned from the doorway. "Y'all relax. I'll come get y'all in about ten minutes," she said and then she slammed the door!

Gabi lifted sarcastic eyes to his. "They do it up nice for their judges, don't they?"

"Funny," he grunted. The fact that he was locked in a closet with a beautiful woman was not lost on Jess. Not after thinking about kissing her for nearly a week now. It was all he could do to fight off the urge to lean closer—not that getting any closer was an option. He'd missed seeing her. He'd almost tripped himself up getting across the room to talk to her when she'd walked in. And his knees were feeling kinda wobbly and this time it had nothing to do with seeing his own blood.

He was standing with his shoulder touching the door while she was facing the door with her shoulder touching his chest. She turned suddenly in the tight space and caught him with his nose practically buried in her hair.

"Um, you smell great," he blurted.

Her eyes, as green as a polished apple, held his. "If you'd have smelled me earlier, I can promise you, after what I did to sixty head of cattle today, you wouldn't have been pleased to be locked inside a football stadium with me."

He laughed. "Then I guess today is my lucky day."

Her lips curved into a smile, that dimple saying hello. She glanced pointedly about the closet. "Now that depends on how you look at it."

Oh, he was looking at it all right. Looking

at her. They were face-to-face and six inches apart. He had room to back up or move sideways, but he stayed put. Feet planted firmly where they were.

He'd thought about her all week. Couldn't shake her from his thoughts no matter how much he tried.

Jess wasn't much into chick flicks but he'd seen a few, and there had been plenty of dramatic long pauses where the camera moved in close as the two main characters stared longingly into each other's eyes. Until this moment he'd thought that was just plain weird.

But he'd felt the same way in the woods. He fought off the overwhelming urge to wrap his arms around Gabi and kiss her—just like in the movies.

What was going on?

The question jolted through him. *What is going on?*

The reality of the situation had him trying to step back. Gabi did, too.

Before either of them could say anything, Norma Sue yanked the door open.

If his expression was anything like Gabi's, they both looked like deer caught in the headlights.

"Okay, judges. Do your thing," Norma Sue

demanded, grinning at Jess like she knew exactly what he'd been thinking about.

Which of course she couldn't know.

Jess needed space. He didn't want to fall for Gabi.

Storming to the table, he sank into the metal folding chair and stared at the twenty small paper cups of various colored cobblers. Even the temptation of berry cobbler couldn't clear his head.

His stomach rolled, his palms were sweating, his nerves shaken. He had never—and he meant *never* had a reaction like the one he'd just had inside that closet with Gabi Newberry. Every time he was around her this thing, this attraction, got bigger and bigger. It was taking on a life of its own.

Jess put a spoonful of entry number six into his mouth, closed his eyes and savored the blackberry cobbler. He looked as if he'd just stepped through the pearly gates.

Gabi had to laugh. "I can see why they want you to do this. You are having entirely too much fun."

He popped one eye open and grinned. "I look forward to this all year long. And I can tell you the benefits aren't bad either." His other eye popped open. "I get cobbler samples all through the year."

"Get out of here," Gabi gasped. "You take bribes?"

He looked insulted. "Not bribes. Just preliminary taste testing." He shrugged. "All I do is thank everyone and eat the pie."

"But then you probably know whose pie you're eating right now."

A wide, closed-lipped smile spread across his lips.

"It's true!" Gabi leaned toward him and hissed, "Do *they* know you know whose pie you're eating?"

"Are you kidding? I'm not certain myself, because they're always tweaking their recipes. Even if I was positive, it wouldn't influence me. Besides, it takes two votes to pick a winner and there is usually someone new helping me every year. This year you're in the hot seat."

"I didn't expect it to be so hard."

"What's hard about it? You get to eat pie and enjoy my great company."

This was impossible!

He was too cute. The way he said it, the way he made a mocking face. He was just plain adorable—and she didn't mean like a puppy! She'd started out with a major hiccup where

Jess was concerned, keeping in perspective that any attraction between them could never go anywhere. She was glad she'd found out his history and views on alcohol. That helped her maintain perspective. If she hadn't known it, she could be in real trouble.

"Great company? Where?" She looked right then left and then back at him with an unimpressed expression.

"Hey, even if you aren't thinking I'm great company, I think you're fantastic."

Gabi's heart missed a beat. It was becoming a common occurance.

"After all the time you spent taking blood samples and looking for poison plants, I'd be a fool not to think you were awesome."

Her heart dropped with surprising force. As if she'd been hoping he really, truly thought she was fantastic or awesome in a more personal way. "You sure would be, buster." She managed a teasing quip. "Thank goodness I love my job."

Taking another bite of cobbler, he closed his eyes. "I love my job, too."

Gabi's stomach felt weak. She swallowed hard and snagged a cup of her own. "But, um, seriously. You don't hear grief when it's all said and done from the ones who didn't win?"

"Nope. They just try harder next year."

"Meaning you get more pie."

His grin bloomed. "Oh, yeah. It's a win-win situation."

"You are living the high life, aren't you?"

He scraped his spoon along the edge of the nearly empty container. "You bet. And luvin' every minute of it."

Gabi couldn't help it. She propped her elbow on the table, dropped her head into her hand and laughed so hard her shoulders shook. That cute smile and happy-go-lucky persona could only get him so far in life. It was the love of berry cobbler that was the secret to life. Or so it seemed for Jess.

Then it hit her. She looked up, met his gaze and suddenly felt very sad. This was a guy whose mother ran out on him and his brothers at an early age. She bet he never got many homemade goodies during his childhood.

All this berry attention probably filled a void in him...and he might not even realize it.

An unexpected tug of emotion waylaid Gabi.

How could a mother do that?

Suddenly there was a yelling commotion from outside.

From the edge of the pavilion, Norma Sue hollered. "Heads up, we got us a loose cannon!"

Jess, as quick as lightning, was already moving, heading for the large opened doors. Gabi followed close at his heels.

"It's a runaway," Esther Mae squealed, flapping her arms, pointing at the huge heifer charging up the hill.

Kids scrambled like ants trying to get out of the way. Cowboys who could have tried to stop the animal were pulling children to safety instead. Obviously the heifer had knocked over some livestock pens, because chickens were everywhere, clambering underfoot and in the air among the plumes of dust stirred up by the excited heifer.

Gabi jumped ahead of the women standing outside the doorway.

"Move to the side of the building," Jess hollered at everyone.

Ignoring Jess's warning and thinking of the older ladies hustling behind her toward safety, Gabi planted her feet, placing herself squarely between the ladies and the oncoming locomotive. What was wrong with this heifer?

Just when Jess thought he had things under control so he could catch frantic heifer, out of the corner of his eye he saw Gabi plant her feet beside him.

"What are you doing? Get out of the way," he yelled.

"No way," Gabi yelled back.

"Woman!" he roared, distracted as he dove for the lead rope swinging from the heifer's halter. The animal charged past him, straight toward the empty building.

"Haya!" Gabi boomed, waving her arms. She ran diagonally behind him, placing herself between the open garage door of the pavilion and the heifer. "Get on outta here."

Jess saw disaster in the making.

"That's the way to do it, Gabi!" someone— Esther Mae it sounded like—yelled.

Jess dove for Gabi, hooked one arm around her waist and lifted her off the ground as he spun them out of the heifer's path.

Nothing stopping it, the animal charged through the door and into the cobbler exhibition!

Blood rushed to Jess's head, he was so angry.

"Woman, are you crazy?" he roared, over the sound of glass shattering, tables flying and metal chairs being stomped. "That could be you that animal is pulverizing."

"Me?" Gabi yelled back, struggling to free herself from his tight grasp. "Together, we could have stopped it from going in there, you big buffoon!"

"Maybe *I* could have but *I* was too busy trying to save *you*."

Thankfully, some other cowboys had reached them and ran inside among the clanging and banging that was going on.

"Put me down," Gabi demanded.

"You were about to get yourself killed, again," Jess snapped, seeing red as he set Gabi down. Tempers flying, they glared at each other in an all-out standoff.

Men! Gabi's adrenaline was flowing as she watched Jess in open-mouthed shock. How dare he?

A huge crash reverberated through the building and several male voices could be heard yelling. Jess glanced over his shoulder at the pavilion then glared at her.

"Stay put." He pointed at the ground beneath her feet.

She ignored him. "I can help. Would you get in there and stop worrying about me—" the words weren't out of her mouth before the heifer charged back outside, *covered* in gooey cobbler!

Jess lunged for the rope, snagged it. The hyped-up cow resisted and Gabi grabbed onto the rope with Jess. It was slick with sticky, slimy berry cobbler and hard to hold onto—obviously the reason the other cowboys couldn't contain it. Together they held it while Jess snagged the halter and held on as the other cowboys came to help.

They finally got the animal subdued and the other men led it off to its pen.

"What were you doing?" Jess asked turning toward her the instant the heifer was gone.

"Helping, that's what." Disgusted, Gabi strode up the slight hill away from him.

"Gabi, you don't go jumping in front of angry cattle like that. What were you thinking?"

He sounded like a broken record! She spun on him. "The same thing you were thinking—stopping that heifer before it hurt someone."

"*You* could have been hurt!"

"So could you. You jumped in front of it because you knew you could stop it or slow it down. I could have, too."

They stared at each other in yet another standoff.

"Gabi," Esther Mae gasped, coming up with Norma Sue, Adela and Rose. "I thought you were going to get ran over. Jess, you were so brave grabbing her up like that."

"I didn't need rescuing, Esther Mae," she ground out trying not to lose patience.

"Looked like it from where we were standing," Norma Sue drawled. Ranch woman that she was, Norma Sue lived in jeans or overalls, today it was overalls and as she spoke she looped her hands around the straps and rolled back on the heels of her boots.

"Where were y'all standing?" Gabi asked, dryly. "I have legs. I have good reflexes."

Giving up, Gabi marched away to look at the damage inside the building. Tables and chairs were upturned about the room. Berry juice and cobbler was all over everything.

"Yikes," she said.

"Whoa," Jess whistled, coming to a halt beside her. Gasps rippled about the crowd gathering beside them.

"Oh my," Adela gasped from behind Gabi.

It looked like the food fight of all food fights had taken place.

"What a mess." Norma Sue grimaced, clapping Jess on the back. "I don't guess y'all got the winner of the contest decided before the world turned upside down, did y'all?"

Chapter Eleven

Jess had picked up feed at Pete's Feed and Seed. Talk at the feed store was on the drought conditions, and the worry that his plant problem could spread across the county. Everyone was watching his situation with interest. Like Gabi had said, drought conditions caused odd situations with plants that normally would be stable. Prussic acid and nitrate poisoning of some kind was likely the cause. Just which plant or plants was it coming from?

There was also talk of the crazy heifer that had crashed the cobbler contest, effectively canceling the competition—Jess had headed home on that note…he was still miffed at Gabi about her actions on that sticky situation.

He was in his office after lunch when Gabi drove up to the small office outside the main barn of his ranch. He'd been on the phone with the last of two calls from cattle buyers arranging for him to transport cattle when he saw her car drive through the gate. Stubborn to the edge of irresponsible, Jess had been put out by Gabi's careless risk. Yes, he reminded himself, she dealt with cattle all the time. Maybe he was feeling overprotective of her. And maybe not. One thing was certain—today was going to be interesting.

The phone rang again as he was getting out of his chair. Grabbing it, he hoped it was a quick call.

"H and H Ranch," he said, distracted by watching Gabi close her truck door.

"Hello, Jess. It…it's your mother. Do you have a minute?"

His hand tightened on the phone, the temptation to hang up strong. It bothered him that the anger he had for his mother still affected him this way. When she was around he managed to be cordial, but he would be lying if he said he wasn't glad she wasn't around all that much.

"Hello, Rhonda. I'm heading out the door," he said, feeling a twinge of guilt. Why should he feel guilty when she'd been the one familiar with walking out the door? Raking his hand through his hair, he hung his head. "What do you need?"

There was a long pause. "I don't need any-thing, Jess. I called to—"

Gabi knocked on the door. Since she could see him through the glass window, there was nothing for him to do but wave her inside.

"—to see if you're going to be in town in two weeks on Saturday," Rhonda was saying as Gabi walked in. "I was hoping to spend some time with you. And, maybe talk before I come down the following week for the rodeo."

Talk. Spend time with me. His instinct was to say, "A little too late for that." But for Luke and Colt's sake, he didn't. "I'll be around." The words were dry, terse, as he was waylaid by the memory of him as a kid, praying that "Rhonda" would come home. Spend time with him. Be what she was supposed to be to him. His mother.

"Good. I'll see you then."

"Yeah, okay, well, I need to go." When she was around, he usually held his emotions in check. The unexpected call surprised him and had his feelings all roiled up.

And then there was Gabi, standing just inside the door.

"Hey," he said, feeling irritable as he hung up. "I guess we're ready then."

"I guess. Bad call?"

Frowning, he snagged his Stetson from the hat rack beside the door.

"Sorry, I shouldn't have asked that."

He shrugged. "Not a problem. Let's hit the trail. I've been cooped up in here for the last hour on the phone and need some fresh air."

"Well, as long as you like it hot, then you're in luck."

"Right now," he said, unable to curb his exasperation, "I'll take fresh air and space any way I can get it." He held the door for Gabi, the scent of her apple shampoo ratcheting up his exasperation.

"You aren't planning on throwing yourself in the path of my bulls today are you?" he drawled sarcastically, hiking a brow when she looked sharply at him.

"Funny," Gabi huffed. "If I feel the urge, who knows what I'll do." Still ticked off by his attitude from the night before, she was more curious than she should be about what she'd walked in on just now.

Jess didn't bother to throw a comeback at her. Instead he grunted again and got in the truck.

The man was clearly irritated—reminding her a little of herself last night after the very eventful day they'd been put through. Her emotions and her patience had been stretched to the limit by Jess's overbearing behavior during the rampaging heifer fiasco.

And now they were spending the afternoon together.

Her first thought was that his bad mood was from the unsettled 'thing' happening between them, but her intuition told her that it was the call he'd been on when she had walked in. The expression on his face when she'd first looked through the window at him had been strained.

She decided to get down to business and not get personal today. "The toxicology report came in this morning."

"And?"

"It *is* nitrate poising, which we pretty much had already figured out. But the problem is we still don't know which plant, the necropsy didn't reveal that. But no worries, because we can find it. We just need to step-up our effort."

He slowed to a stop in the center of the pasture. Gabi wasn't sure if the crunching sound beneath the tires was the gravel or the dry crackly grass. Even in the short time she'd been here, the grass had grown crisper and brown. The temperature had been over one hundred degrees for almost sixty days in a row. No wonder the cattle were eating things they weren't supposed to.

"So what's the plan of action?"

"Susan wants to send samples of your plants to Texas Diagnostic Laboratory in College Station. She's afraid we're about to have cattle dropping all over the county. So there's even more urgency to this than for just your ranch."

Jess stared out over the pasture, as if envisioning the catastrophe. "Talk is that everyone is edgy with the drought conditions settling in like they are. And then that little teaser of rain we've been getting is only setting up perfect conditions for more toxicity levels to show up. Right?"

"Exactly," she answered. "So we're going to gather more samples of the various plants we've already found and any others that we might find. Today I'm going to sketch out and label your land into quadrants. Then bright and early Monday morning I'll begin to cut plants about four inches from the ground, bag them, put them on ice and by three in the afternoon have them in the overnight mail to the College Station lab. They'll tell us specifically which plants in which quadrants have toxic nitrate levels."

"Then what?"

"We can go from there." Gabi thought Jess sounded distracted at first but now was coming around. She was glad. She wasn't about to analyze him too closely. She was fairly certain that the phone conversation she'd walked in on had been strained. A girlfriend, maybe?

One who was probably having trouble taking orders from him. Almost instantly Gabi rejected that idea. Jess didn't act like a man who was tethered to anyone. But something was on his mind. Maybe it was worry about his cattle. Maybe he was mad at her still.

"Are you okay?" The question came out before she could stop it. "I get the feeling something's wrong. Are you aggravated at me still for trying to help corral that heifer?" She decided to be direct.

"Are you kidding? You were right," he drawled, sarcasm in his tone. "You work with animals all the time and are completely qualified to throw yourself in front of oncoming heifers all you want."

Gabi didn't let him get to her. "I was fine."

"Look, Gabi. I'd tell you that I won't do it again, but that'd be a lie. If I see you are about to step on a snake, or a fifteen-hundred-pound heifer is about to run over you, I'm going to pull you out of the danger zone. End of story."

Steam clouded Gabi's vision but she exhaled to calm herself and spoke carefully. "As long as you don't think I can't take care of myself. I don't mind letting a man sweep in and save the day. Just don't go thinking I couldn't have helped you out. And don't go telling me when and what to do."

"You've got a hang-up where needing help is concerned."

Her mouth dropped open. "I didn't *need* to be rescued. I don't mind that you reacted like you did because you couldn't help yourself. But I didn't need you." There was no talking to this man. According to him, she'd messed up and he'd been perfect. Uggg, it was enough to make a girl yank out her ponytail. *Search me, O God, and know my heart; test me and know my anxious thoughts.* The verse from her morning Bible reading sprang into her thoughts.

"Fine, you didn't need me," Jess snapped, glaring at her.

They stared at each other for a long moment. Gabi had a problem thinking straight while looking at the handsome, exasperating man. It wasn't fair—the man was more attractive now than before! How was that possible?

"We have a standoff," he muttered at last.

"Don't we always?" Gabi snapped. "But we also have work to be done."

His mouth edged into a smile. "How about if you let me save you, as long as I know that you could have done it on your own. And you can save me when I need it. Like you're doing with these toxic plants—on that front, I need you to save me and I'll readily admit it."

She sighed. "Who could refuse an offer like that?"

As exasperating as the man was, the butterflies in Gabi's stomach seemed oblivious as his eyes lightened and met hers.

"So," Jess asked, gruffly, frowning. "Where do you want to start? The sooner we get this done, the better all around."

Gabi jerked herself away from where her thoughts were heading. This was business.

Business.

But goodness, Jess Holden had a way, even when he was grumpy and overbearing, of making her toes tingle.

And that was just plain aggravating.

Waves of heat rose like invisible steam from underbrush banking the stream running through the woods. Jess blinked against the salty sting of sweat rolling into his eyes.

Eyes he'd worked hard to keep off of Gabi all afternoon. How did she do it? The temperature hovered at one-hundred-and-five degrees, but despite the heat she was relentless in drawing an in-depth grid of his pastures and the plants they needed to harvest for the toxicology lab. Respect for Gabi slowly edged out his bad mood over the phone call from Rhonda, and even over Gabi's habit of putting herself in harm's way. He focused on solving his current problem versus the issues of his past.

Gabi's dedication had been amazing when it was just his cattle that were in danger. Now, with the threat of problems spreading across the county, she'd stepped it up even more. A seriousness flowed from her while she surveyed and sketched.

Despite his struggle not to, watching Gabi helped take the edge off the emotions Rhonda's call had brought up in him.

Shelving old feelings like he'd always done and getting on with his life had been a promise he'd made to himself when he was a teenager. But today, something had happened when he'd heard Rhonda's voice. Pushing the thoughts away once more, he strode to the edge of the stream. Normally the water was over the tops of his boots in this particular spot. Now, it wouldn't cover the top of his instep if he walked into the center of the barely flowing water.

There was no breeze today, making the air as thick and as shallow of oxygen as the stream was of water.

Sweat beaded on Gabi's brow and glistened off her burnished shoulders. The hair about her face curled damply and even her ponytail seemed to droop in the heat.

Still, she worked.

His gut tightened, and he tried not to let his thoughts get personal. Pulling a bottle of water from his backpack, he headed her way. Maybe it was the heat, because nothing seemed to help.

"Gabi, drink this," he urged, determined to take care of her. Knowing they'd be out in this heat today, he'd prepared an ice cooler of water and had it ready in the truck before she'd arrived. She worked for him and he felt responsible—whether she wanted him to or not. "I don't want you getting overheated like you did the other day."

She finished drawing then poked her pencil behind her ear before placing the notebook under her elbow. Taking the bottle from him, her eyes met his.

Was it his imagination or did she carefully avoid his touch as she took the water? The idea that she was just as aware of what happened when they touched had his adrenaline running the high line. Caution lights flashed in his head and he knew, if he wasn't careful, something told him he might hit the wall on this one.

He needed to focus on the reason his cattle were dying. Not on the beautiful vet assistant.

Maybe it *was* the heat making him feel so reckless. One minute he was standing there telling himself to hit the brakes and the next, he lifted his hand and gently touched her temple.

Gabi froze—which he wasn't sure was any better than if she'd stepped away from him. But that didn't stop him.

"Have I told you how much I appreciate all the work you've been doing?"

"Yes. You have." She said the words carefully. "But there isn't any need. I'm happy to do it."

What was it he was seeing in her eyes? He knew she was as attracted to him as he was to her. He stepped closer, drawn to her. He let his finger slide down to her chin, tilting it up. He was giving her the opportunity to move away, if he was misreading the signs. His heart thundered—Dale Earnhardt Jr. had nothing on him. What was it about Gabi that did this to him?

His gaze dropped to her lips and his gut clenched.

"Jess," Gabi breathed his name, her heart pounding from the way he was looking at her. She told herself not to get too excited. Jess was a beautiful man, handsome beyond belief with a personality that rode roughshod over any man she'd ever met. She should feel flattered that he was thinking about kissing her...and there was no doubt in her mind that he was.

Guilt, sharp as the thorn that had impaled his finger the week before, stabbed her. She knew his history and knew there was no future here. She'd done something horrible, and she knew when Jess learned her secret, his opinion of her would change.

She backed away from him, squeezing the water bottle he'd given her to her chest like a shield between them. "I need to tell you something."

She did not want to tell Jess what she'd done. The very idea had her stomach tied in knots, but it was the right thing to do. This thing between them had gone way too far.

She wouldn't deceive him when she knew in her heart how differently he would feel about her once he knew the truth.

The heat sucked her in, and the forest shifted about her. Shadows deepened, and the swirl of colors spun in her head as worry danced with the heat sucking her energy and will. She'd wanted Jess to like her—the knowledge shook her. But she couldn't mislead him.

She couldn't.

She had more integrity than that. So it was confession time.

"Did you know I was engaged up until a month ago?"

His teal blue eyes watched her beneath brows etched with…concern? Disbelief?

"I knew. What had happened?"

"Phillip broke it off. I know now, it was the best thing." She frowned, realizing again how very true that was. "But what I need to tell you is that I…" She paused, not letting herself back down. "Jess there's no other way to say this except that I got drunk at a party one night, got in my car and had a terrible wreck."

His jaw had tensed and his expression hardened. She knew he was probably thinking the worst of her.

"I ended up in the emergency room with basically minor injuries, especially considering that my car was so destroyed that I shouldn't have walked away alive."

"Was anyone else injured?" His words were quiet, echoing in the stillness of the woods.

Gabi shook her head. "No. But only by God's grace," she admitted. "There was a car full of teenagers who managed to swerve and miss me. I hit a concrete wall head-on instead."

"Thank God."

"Yes. It *was* God. That's all it could be. He had his hand on everyone and protected us all."

Tears threatened and she blinked them away, remembering her blessing in all of this.

"Jess. Sometimes the most horrible thing in your life can turn out to be the best thing. A beautiful thing, even. And that's the way it was for me."

"How is that?" Distance had crept into the mix like an unwelcome third wheel.

She took a deep breath. "The thing is, my being drunk was a common occurrence. My life had become one party after the other. Phillip was a musician, and I was just absorbed into his lifestyle."

Jess crossed his arms, jaw still tensed. Gabi's heart fluttered at the picture of him closing a door between them.

She knew it was about to get worse. "When you talked about your dad, I got sick thinking that if I hadn't had my eyes opened I...I could have become an alcoholic too." Her voice faded and guilt churned in her stomach.

"You sound certain about that. How so?" Distaste rang in his question like a slap to her face.

Gabi licked her lips searching for moisture. "Because, I liked it too much. They say that all it takes is one drink and some people are hooked." Her hands shook, the water bottle trembled so she dropped her hand to her side and tried to hide it. "That was me. I wasn't hooked," she denied. "But well on my way to being out of control.

"Once I started drinking, I didn't slow down. My mom worried about me all the time. She didn't tell Gram that she suspected that I was in trouble until a few months ago. She was at her wit's end and needed Gram to pray for me."

Gabi'd wanted to keep this in her past, but once she'd started talking it was just pouring out. And to Jess, who of all people had the most reason of anyone to look down at her.

"So what happened?" He walked a few feet away, distancing himself.

Gabi took a long breath, feeling unexplainable sadness at the look in his eyes. "A nurse at the hospital got real with me. She'd lost her son to a drunk driver and she made me aware of how devastated she was and how close I came to wiping out a car full of teenagers. She called me to the mat on it. Hard. Told me about how it felt to lose a son and how it still hurt and always would. Judy told me she worked E.R. just so she could talk to people like me. That it was her purpose now to share God with me and others like me." Gabi stood and paced, feeling those words to the depth of her soul. "*Like me.* That was a tough one. I didn't want to be 'like me' in that moment. I was so sick to my stomach over what I'd nearly done. I will never forget the clarity of shame I felt in that moment of realization." The look of disgust edging into Jess's eyes had her stomach roiling even as the guilt ate at her.

"Thinking that I could have killed someone makes me ill, even now. I heard Judy loud and clear and opened my eyes. And changed my ways. I thank God every day for sparing those kids."

"He spared you, too." His words surprised her.

"Yes, but that's secondary. I'll never forget the look on Judy's face, when she spoke about losing her son." Gabi wrapped her arms across her body as an icy shiver raced through her. "When you talked about your dad, I had this horrible thought that I could have married Phillip, had children, and you could have been my son one day talking about me."

Jess tugged at his ear, studied his boots before finally hitting her with frank eyes. "I'm glad you made the right choice. There are too many parents making the wrong choices these days. You can bet that if I ever do decide to marry and have kids, like Luke wants me to do, there won't be any chance at all that my kids will *ever* have to deal with an alcoholic."

His adamant declaration hung between them

like a warning sign. His passion gave her no doubt that what he said was true. The heat of the day had nothing on the heat of emotion radiating from him.

Gabi was relieved. But he'd said *if...if I marry and have kids like Luke wants me to.* Gabi was saddened by that. Had Jess's childhood scarred him deep enough that he wasn't considering marriage and children at all?

The idea hit her so wrong that she couldn't bring herself to ask more...the man had said it all, hadn't he?

"So, what about these plants?" His sudden change of subject was like a dead bolt slamming shut on the door he'd just closed between them.

She squared her shoulders, despite her damaged pride. She'd done this to herself, and now these were the consequences for her actions. God didn't say all things were good. He said He could make good come from bad situations. But what good could come from this?

"You're right," she said, glad when her voice sounded halfway normal. "We have work to do and solutions to find."

Jess nodded, strode to the woods and began studying the underbrush.

Gabi watched with a heavy heart.

What good, Lord, can come from this?

Chapter Twelve

"Have you asked her out yet?"

Jess propped his boot on the lower rung of Murdock's stall, hung his elbows on a mid-rung and studied the horse that was winning its way to becoming a national champion in women's barrel racing. Jess had tossed and turned all night. He'd finally climbed out of bed at daybreak and ridden across the pastures thinking about Gabi…and his past. He'd ended up here, at Luke's, and found him tending to Murdock before going inside to get ready for church.

Luke had taken one look at Jess and asked his question.

Hiding his interest in Gabi from his brother was obviously not happening. But did it matter? He'd come here for advice.

"No, I haven't."

Luke hung his elbows on the rung beside

him, questions in his eyes as he stared at him. "Jess, man, what are you waiting on? You look like you haven't slept all night. What's up?"

"She has a history with drinking, Luke."

The words hung in the barn like the tainted memories of their past. He didn't need to say more.

"I see," Luke grimaced, understanding without words what that meant to Jess. Silently they both studied the horse. Seconds ticked into minutes as Murdock quietly chewed on his hay, totally at ease with being studied.

"You said, a history. Does she have a *problem* with it?"

"From what she says, she gave it up when she had a near-fatal car wreck. A nurse helped her see how lucky she was not to have killed herself or the carload of kids she ran off the road. She accepted the Lord that night and turned over a new leaf."

"But you don't believe her."

"It's not that I don't believe her. It's, well, you know the old song and dance. How many times did we hear that from our dad. I'm giving up the alcohol, he'd say, slurring words because never did he say them when he was sober. Only when he was totally wasted—crying-in-his-beer-feel-sorry-for-me wasted." Jess's grip tightened on the rail, his stomach rolling with lost hope. "There was never any chance that he would really do it," he finished in disgust. But as a kid it had been pain he'd felt. Pain and loss.

"You can't judge everyone by him, Jess."

"No, I shouldn't. But when it comes to my personal life choices, you bet I can. And I do. And I will."

Luke raked a hand through his dark, wavy hair which was similar to Jess's. They'd inherited their hair and looks from their dad. Colt had sandy-brown hair, more like their mother's. Luke and Colt had also inherited their mother's brown eyes. Jess didn't even have that reprieve when he looked in the mirror. Every day he saw his dad's face and his dad's ocean-blue eyes staring back at him. It was a reminder to Jess of the man he never wanted to be—ever.

And that meant Jess made choices all the time to avoid reminders of his dad's life choices. "You know I don't drink, never touched the stuff and never date anyone who does. I'm certainly not going to date someone who just told me she had a problem with it."

"She told you that? Just came out and said she did?"

He shot Luke a disbelieving glare. "She almost killed herself and a load of kids she was so drunk. Yes, she said the words."

Luke stared at his boots for a minute. When

he finally looked up there was regret in his eyes. "That's too bad, Jess. I understand how you feel. I hate it, but I understand." He straightened and stuffed his hands in his pockets. "I want to tell you to let God lead you. To let go of the past—but I know how hard that is for you. I can tell you that God can work all things out. I've seen it over and over and over. And if you'll just trust Him, give this over to Him, He'll show you the way."

Jess straightened, suddenly feeling as if his emotions were filleted open, raw and bare. "On this issue, I don't need to be shown the way."

Disappointment clung to Luke like the worrisome buffalo gnats hovering about them. "I get where you're at, but Gabi isn't Dad. I don't think you need to judge her by his mistakes. I heard y'all hit it off for a while there at the fair."

"Luke, I've never told you this because I didn't want to disappoint you after all you did for me and Colt growing up. This ranch, this dream you have for it to be a legacy...I'm here with you. But as for me falling in love and living happily ever after like you're trying to do—"

"I know, you told me you weren't the commitment type. But maybe, you are and just don't know it."

Luke, ever positive, was trying hard. Jess

shook his head. "It's more than that, Luke. I'm not sure I even believe in love. Not for me anyway." Frustration, disappointment, disbelief—yeah, disbelief was the strongest emotion Jess read in Luke's expression.

"I'm not *attempting* a happily ever after, Jess. I'm living it. And you can, too."

"No, I can't. I don't think I'm capable of trusting my future to someone else."

Luke's expression turned doubtful. "I'm not following you."

"Falling in love with someone would mean I trust them with my happiness. And I don't trust that to anyone anymore but me."

It was the hard-learned truth.

"You don't know what you're missing. Look, I need to get inside and clean up. Montana is going to think I don't want to go to church with her." He grinned, surprising Jess. "You keep thinking that way and I can promise you you'll miss out on the best thing that could ever happen to you. I don't know what I ever did without Montana. Why don't you come to chur—"

Jess stopped Luke before he could ask. "I'm heading home. I've got a load of cattle to pick up all the way over in Centerville around two, then transport back up this way."

"You couldn't have made that trip tomorrow and come to church today? I wish you'd—"

Jess cut him off once more. "I'm working here tomorrow with Gabi bagging up samples and shipping them overnight down to College Station to the lab."

"Do you want me to do that for you? I mean, if it's bothering you to be around Gabi."

"Your plate is full enough. Besides, I'm no quitter. Just because I'm not planning on marrying Gabi Newberry doesn't mean I can't work with her."

"Sounds like a plan to me." Luke chuckled then sauntered off toward the house.

Jess watched him go, then headed for his horse. Why did everyone think they had it all figured out? He sure didn't. And working with Gabi this coming week did not sound like a plan to him. It was just the way it had to be. The dead cattle were his, so he would be there by Gabi's side till the solution was found. And when this was done, they'd go their separate ways. And that was a promise.

Gabi figured they'd had a good day. She and Jess had managed to make it through Monday without her having a breakdown, Jess passing out or hurting himself, or any other new mishap that seemed to happen to them when they were out in the field working together.

She'd also kept her mouth shut. She'd learned

her lesson on Saturday and had no urge today to tell Jess more of her entire sordid past. *What had she been thinking?*

The man clearly was uncomfortable with her today. But so was she with him. Who wouldn't be after airing their dirty laundry? Needless to say, with eggshells seemingly crunching beneath their boots, they'd stuck strictly to business, gathering up the varying plants and then placing them in the Ziploc bags.

"It's hard to believe that all those are samples of toxic plants."

Some of them were so tall they had to be folded over and placed in garbage bags. When they had them all boxed up on the first day, it was a good-sized box they were sending the lab.

"And there's more to go," Gabi added, watching the delivery truck disappear down the lane from the office. Thankfully they'd been able to arrange for the truck to pick up the samples rather than them driving all the way to Ranger.

With the plants done for the day and nothing else to concentrate on, Gabi was ready to get home and away from Jess. It had been a hard day. He'd said nothing about her confession to him. And though she'd expected her past to put a wall between them, she hadn't expected that it would bother her so much when he ignored it.

She should never have opened up to him.

She'd promised herself on coming to Mule Hollow that she would start fresh. That she didn't have to tell anyone about her past and she wasn't going to. A clean slate. Wasn't that what God had done for her? So why, oh why, had she suddenly spilled everything to Jess?

Hurrying to her truck, she'd packed up her things in a matter of seconds and had her hand on the door ready to make her escape.

"Thanks for all your hard work," Jess said.

She glanced over her shoulder. "You're welcome. But it's my job." Her words came off sounding strained.

"Right. Business." His words came off sounding sarcastic.

It irritated her that he repeated the word as if it was a shock that she was trying to stay professional. After all, he was the one who'd touched her. He was the one who had clammed up after she'd revealed her past to him.

Her fault. Her fault. Her fault!

Gabi was not blaming this on anyone else. She'd gotten too personal. And he obviously was uncomfortable with it. Or he just thought the worst of her.

"See you later, Jess. I need to get back to work at the clinic. I'll be back out tomorrow."

"I'll be here."

Yeah, right, Gabi thought as she left. She'd be glad when the job was done.

And that was the truth.

Jess was having a horrible week. It was the plain, hard truth.

It didn't feel right keeping Gabi at arm's length. He didn't understand why it felt so wrong, but it did.

He'd had to work beside her all week, and keeping his mind off her and how pretty she looked in the morning light, the noonday light, the afternoon's harsh hot light was impossible!

She was driving him nuts.

And more so since she was totally ignoring the fact that they'd shared intimate details of their past lives.

Yes, he didn't like her past. But she'd shared it with him. And he was pretty certain no one else in town knew all the details. Maybe not even her grandmother, Adela.

The thought gnawed at him…. Gabi had trusted him enough with her difficult past.

He didn't want to ask more, but like a drunk in the living room, it lay there between them and could be ignored but not unseen.

"Are you all right?" Gabi asked Jess the next morning. They'd gathered plants from most of the pastures and only had a few places left to explore. Despite her determination to not think about him other than as a client, she was finding it impossible.

Those deep aqua eyes of his had her thinking of lazy days by the beach—not so hard to imagine since they were sweltering in what was now being predicted would be the hottest summer drought in years for Texas.

That heat was to blame for much of her insanity when they were together. At least that was another thing she tried to convince herself of.

"Sure, I'm fine."

Gabi paused sealing the baggie with a sample of Conyza. Though this plant was known to kill livestock during drought, it was extremely unpalatable and only eaten when there was nothing else. She doubted very seriously that this was Jess's problem. Besides that, one of the symptoms prior to death was cattle walking in circles. Since all of Jess's cattle seemed to be walking fine, Gabi was only sending the sample off because she wasn't taking any chances.

"If you say so, but you seem distracted, and if you're not careful with those shears, you're going to chop off a finger or something." They'd been tiptoeing around each other for days, but today seemed different. Or maybe she was just tired of them talking but not really talking. And she'd been thinking about how she'd wanted to try and help him. Foolish on her part.

The disbelief in Jess's expression, that she would even imply he might cut off his finger, was priceless.

"I am *not* going to chop my finger off."

"Most people who do it didn't plan on it beforehand." She hiked a brow.

His eyes narrowed. "Seriously, I am not one of them."

"That's good since you'd pass out at the sight of your own blood and bleed to death before help could get here. So I guess if it should happen it's a good thing I'm here."

"Seriously," he said, and then laughed when she did.

"So really, what's the matter? Does it have to do with me?"

He tucked his chin, then hit her with those beachcombing eyes. "It's my mother."

"Your *mother?*"

"I told you she disappeared when I was ten, and now she's trying to get back into my life. She called again today."

They were standing at the back of the truck with the tailgate down, using it as a work station for getting the plants ready to ship. Gabi leaned her hip against it and gave him her full attention. "This is something new?"

"Not really."

Suddenly it hit her. "She called you last week, didn't she?"

"Yup, how did you know?"

"You looked similarly frustrated last week when I came to the office."

"Yeah, that'd be the day. Had her and you both to deal with."

The fact that he was able to tease her gave Gabi a thrill that she ignored. Instead she shot him a saucy look as she folded over a long bundle of horseweed and placed it inside a medium-size garbage bag.

"She's coming Saturday to the rodeo to watch Colt and wants to talk."

"Clearly you have a problem with this."

Jess paced back and forth by the tailgate. "I'm dealing with her coming back into my life, through Luke and Colt. They both somehow have been able to look past what she did and forgive her."

"But not you."

His eyes were as cold and sharp as the blue on the tip of an Alaskan iceberg. "Maybe it was my age. Luke was almost a man, Colt was too little to know what he was missing. I was ten."

Gabi's heart ached anew for the little boy who'd been so hurt by his parents' problems and ultimate betrayal. "You needed her very much at that age," she said, simply.

"And now she expects me to forgive her."

Gabi didn't miss that he hadn't acknowledged out loud that he'd needed his mother. "Maybe she's changed."

"I'm thinking that'd be a correct assessment from her view of the situation. She can leave when she wants and come back when she wants. Isn't that convenient?"

Gabi didn't know what to say. She studied him thoughtfully. "Forgiving isn't always easy. I guess it probably isn't ever easy. I'm no professional and not sure what my advice is worth, but I'd say do what you need to do."

Dust stirred suddenly and the sound of a truck drew their attention. Instead of the overnight express truck coming as they'd both thought, it was Luke's double cab truck approaching at a fast clip.

"Hi, Gabi," Luke said, the instant he came to a halt. "Everything going the way you want it?"

She pushed away from the tailgate. "Great. We almost have everything tagged and mailed."

Luke gave her an easy grin that looked so much like Jess. They looked a lot alike, except where Jess's eyes were so dazzling blue, Luke's were a rich, coffee brown. "You've kept this one in shape, I guess?" He cocked his head toward Jess.

"Trying to."

"Hey!" Jess exclaimed. "I'm working circles around you."

"Ha. In your dreams, Jesse James," she teased, noticing how easy it was to fall back into an easy banter with Jess.

"I'm no outlaw," he said.

"But you're dangerous—" Gabi said it before she could stop herself. The man *was* dangerous, but only to her!

"Glad you can hold your own," Luke laughed, looking from Jess to her. "Gabi. Look, I'm sorry I haven't been able to help."

"That's okay," she said, glad he moved the conversation forward. "Jess explained he was taking this on while you had to focus on the rodeos. We wouldn't want to mess with the Mule Hollow Homecomings. My Gram and Esther Mae and Norma Sue have worked too hard on them."

Luke agreed. "That's the truth. Look, I came by because Montana is coming home late tonight and wanted me to invite you to dinner tomorrow night while she's in town. She's really looking forward to meeting you, so I was hoping you'd be able to let us thank you proper for all the work you've been doing."

There was no way she could say no. "Sure, I'd love to come have dinner with you and Montana."

Luke's eyes slid to Jess. "Montana expects you, too. She said for you to pick Gabi up. Think you can handle that, Jesse James?" he asked, grinning, his gaze openly teasing his brother.

Jess caught Gabi's eye and held. "I can handle it."

But could she? Gabi wondered, clearly hearing the challenge.

The challenge lingered between them in the sweltering heat. Gabi focused on the positive side…. They'd made it through the week—surely they could make it through dinner.

Chapter Thirteen

"I can handle it." What an idiot. Jess was still thinking about those words after a quick shower and a ham sandwich. Shaking his head on that one, he headed out to the barn and pulled the tarp off his 1961 Chevy.

He'd spent many an hour working on restoring this truck. Those hours had been good therapy when he had had things on his mind. Tonight was no different. "I can handle it, my foot," he grunted thinking about Luke and Montana going matchmaker on him.

Colt was expected to get home sometime the next day and Jess was looking forward to seeing his little brother. Putting his strength behind the wrench, Jess let his frustrations loosen what felt like a cemented connection. He'd not had any peace since Gabi had driven off today. The phone hanging at the barn entrance rang, breaking into his thoughts. Wiping his hands, Jess hurried to pick it up.

"Hello," he grunted.

"What's eat'n you?" Colt chuckled.

"Nothing," Jess lied, which only made Colt laugh more.

"Don't give me that. Sounds like woman trouble to me. What's going on, Jess?"

"You don't want to know," he said.

"Yeah, I do. I might be even half way across Texas but I do want to know. Luke said you were interested in Adela's granddaughter. I'm thinking that's really pushing your luck with the matchmakers."

"Tell me about it. Namely your big brother and his new bride."

"No, say it ain't so. Luke's trying to fix you up?"

Jess told him about the dinner the following night. Colt sighed.

"You know he just wants the best for us."

Jess didn't miss the weariness in Colt's voice despite his interest in what he had to say. "You're exhausted. Why don't you curl up somewhere and take a nap before you finish the road trip home."

"Why don't you not change the subject. Come on, spill. I'm gonna be home before midnight tomorrow night and I'm going to come in and wake you up for the details. I might be the youngest and the shortest but you know I can take you."

Jess knew Colt was grinning as he made the challenge. It was a lifelong good-natured rivalry. Truth was, with Colt's strength, built from years of riding bulls and his speed, Jess wasn't too sure who would win. "So you think," he grunted.

"Spit it out, Jess. I'm out of the loop as it is, so give me a break. Not to mention that I'm about to fall asleep at the wheel and need something to give me a boost."

"What's to tell?"

"Tell me about Gabi."

Jess didn't like hearing how tired Colt was; it wasn't the best way to travel. Jess raked his fingers through his hair. He needed to help Colt wake up and he needed to talk.

"She's fun. She's funny. She knows her own mind and doesn't mind voicing her opinion and I find that attractive."

"So what's got you so bent out of shape?"

How could Jess tell Colt the problem was that she loved the Lord with all her heart and she didn't mind speaking up about it? For him that was uncomfortable. But there was more. "She's had a problem with drinking, Colt."

"That doesn't make her an alcoholic, Jess." Colt zeroed in on Jess's unspoken fear.

"It's close enough for me."

"So, you're going to let the fact that she used to have a problem stop you from—"

Jess's grip tightened on the phone. "You and Luke sound like recordings of each other."

"That's because we're both concerned and want the best for you. Jess, Luke's let go of the past and moved forward. I'm dealing with it better than you, and I was the kid. I was wet behind the ears when Mom left us. Eight years old—old enough to remember things, but I don't. Not much. Except, Dad yelling at me when I broke a bottle of beer, or him wanting me to take a drink and Luke telling me not to *ever* drink. Luke fixing us peanut butter sandwiches. Luke picking me up when I fell off the fence…and telling me that one day things would be better. And you, taking up for me at school when kids made fun of me for the holes in my shoes. Out of all of it, you and Luke are what I remember most."

Conversations like this made Jess's heart go stone-cold. Luke had forgiven their mother for abandoning them because he was a man of honor who wanted to control how he looked at life and not let his circumstances dictate it. Colt, he was harder to peg.

"Look, Colt, I've got to go. Are you awake now?"

"Sure thing. Bright eyed and ready to meet this little gal that's got you twisted into knots. I'll be there before you can steer dog a calf."

Jess frowned into the phone. "You pull over if you get too tired or I'll be steer doggin' you when I see you. And me and Luke are only a phone call away."

"That's not exactly true out there in Mule Hollow with the cell reception being so useless. But I'll stop if I need to. I'm ready to get home for a little while. I'm wore out."

"You've done good though, Colt. Ranking third on the leader board is a great place to be right now. So come home and rest up like Montana is doing. Your body has got to be worn down."

"Yeah. That's what I'm doing. I need the peace and rest at the ranch. I'll see you in a blink, brother."

"Be safe, I'll leave your lights on."

That got him a tired laugh as the line went dead. Tomorrow he'd be heading over to Colt's place and turn all the lights on. When he busted through the trees that separated his little cabin from the world, Colt would see a shining beacon of welcome.

Who was he kidding? Jess could gripe all he wanted but the truth was—he wanted to see Gabi. Was drawn to her. And Luke had given him another excuse to spend time with her.

"Here we are," Jess said the following night as he pulled to a stop in front of Montana and Luke's home.

It was older but neat. Jess smiled usually when he drove into the yard—even though Montana was on the road most of the time, one of the first things she'd done after she and Luke got married was plant welcoming pink periwinkles in front of the hedges that surrounded the house. The place had brightened up after that. But the highlight of the front yard was the crape myrtle tree that stood taller than the house and was in full bloom. Jess liked the look of it. Gabi stopped and took a moment to admire it, too.

"This is amazing." She touched the low-hanging frilly blooms, smiling.

His stomach went bottomless. "Yeah, it is. This tree is one of my favorite things about this place," Jess admitted, trying not to think about how startled he'd been when she'd opened the door with her hair falling loosely down her back and her blouse as frilly as the crape myrtle blossom. But this tree—it had nothing on Gabi.

The drive from Gabi's hadn't been a quiet one. Gabi had begun asking him questions about his mother almost immediately. They'd not gotten to finish their conversation the day before.

He'd been upset with his mother then and needed to vent. Tonight his tongue and brain were all tied up and twisted and it was because of Gabi. Out in the pastures, dressed in her worn jeans and tank tops and her cute little ponytail hanging down her back, she was a knockout, but he'd gotten used to her that way.

If he'd known she was going to let her hair hang loose and her softer side show tonight, he'd have known to be ready to kiss his good sense goodbye.

Plain and simple: he couldn't think straight looking at her right now. *He could handle it.* What a joke.

Gabi Newberry did something to him he'd never experienced before. Oh, his pulse had raced with attraction before, but there was something about Gabi he couldn't get a finger on. There were good reasons he didn't need to let himself begin to find out why she made him feel so alive. And that was exactly what the difference was. When he was around her, he felt vital.

Like he was a part of something that was bigger than him.

"We better go in," he said, fighting the feelings racing through him. "Montana will think I decided to kidnap you or something." He had a long evening ahead of them as he headed toward the house, with Gabi at his side…

A knot formed in his gut. He was going to have to tread lightly. Get through this night then move on. He wasn't stupid. Never had been. He knew a danger zone when he'd entered it.

Gabi was dangerous to him.

"Those were the best fajitas I've ever had," Gabi told Montana as she helped her clear the dishes from the table.

"Thanks, Luke can cook, can't he?"

"Yes, he can. The entire evening was nice."

They'd eaten outside on the patio. After a lively conversation-filled dinner, the guys had gone to the barn, leaving Montana and her alone.

Dishes done, they walked back out onto the porch with glasses of tea, settling into the bright pillow-filled lounge chairs. Montana sank onto one of them, lifted up her feet and let them fall onto the lounger with a thud.

"Goodness, I needed this!" she said. "My schedule for the last month has been grueling. But I'm loving it. I'm living my dream and that includes being married to Luke."

"I hear you're doing great, winning a lot of barrel racing competitions."

"I am, thankfully. If I wasn't, I'd feel guilty taking this much time away from being here. We didn't plan on falling in love, but once we did, it didn't make sense not to go ahead and get married. We had Chance marry us—you've met him, haven't you? Our cowboy preacher at the Mule Hollow Church of Faith?"

Gabi nodded.

"Then we went to a rodeo. I mean really, when your heart and God's word line up in harmony, you know it's right. So why wait?"

Gabi found out during the course of the meal that Montana and Luke had fallen in love very quickly. It had shocked them all, but in the end it had been undeniable that God had brought them together. Gabi loved their story. They saw they were good together. Like Montana said, when everything lines up, all is good in the world.

Gabi thought about that. She knew with more certainty every day that her life with Phillip hadn't lined up with anything, especially the Bible. Being in the clubs where he played each night gave her far too much access to alcohol than she needed. And the women who threw themselves at him didn't help the situation. Opening a little, she told Montana some about her relationship and how grateful she was for the life she was living now.

"There had been nothing about our relationship that had anything to do with Christ's will for my life. The next go round, that's going to be my priority. I see what you and Luke have. And I watch Susan and Cole, my Gram and Sam, and so many couples here in Mule Hollow whose love for each other is as strong as their love for God. And that's what I *have* to have." Gabi knew she needed that kind of love in her life—when she was ready to look again.

"Then you just hang in there, Gabi. Hang in there and see where God takes you. But—" Montana smiled over the brim of her tea glass "—you have to be prepared to be totally surprised about where He takes you."

Gabi was thoughtful for a minute as thoughts and questions bombarded her. "Can I ask you about their parents? You know, Luke, Jess and Colt? Jess seems to have scars that really run deep."

Running her hand over the top of her head to

smooth down a wayward strand of dark brown hair, Montana looked out over the pasture with a troubled expression. When she turned back to Gabi, there was fire in her eyes.

"What their parents did to them makes me *so* mad, Gabi." Her voice thickened with emotions. "I love Luke with all my heart. He's the best man I've ever known, but he's that way *despite* what his parents did to him. Luke's mother deserted them when he was fourteen. She left them in the care of a drunkard dad who couldn't keep work and hardly tried. He'd disappeared into a bottle long before that and never really came out again. Luke opens up more and more about it, but he doesn't dwell on it. At fourteen he took on the responsibility of trying to look out for his little brothers and in many ways his dad, too. He could have been bitter and no count like his dad, but with all of that on his young shoulders Luke chose to be a man of honor." Montana smiled brightly.

"Goodness, I love that man. He helped me with my forgiveness issues that I had with my own father. Can you imagine that? He deserves to be happy and I love that I'm the woman God made to make him happy."

Montana had Gabi's full attention. The passion in her words was unshakable. Gabi wondered what it would be like to feel that. Nope, there was never anything like that between her and Phillip. Gabi definitely wanted a love like this.

And she would wait for it as long as it took to find it.

"I think that's awesome. I want that someday," she said, without going into great detail.

"Jess is a great guy too," Montana continued. "Colt also. But they've all dealt with their past in different ways. Luke wants so badly to fix everything for them. But he can't. Each one of them has his own path to live. Jess is loyal, fun loving, loves his brothers deeply."

"I could tell he was really concerned about the cattle and didn't want to worry Luke if at all possible. As if he wanted to protect him, pay him back for some of all that he'd done for him growing up." Gabi wondered how he felt about being the middle child, watching his family fall apart and then having his older brother be the responsible one. "How old was Jess when Luke started looking out for him?" she couldn't help but ask.

"He was ten and Colt was eight. Luke tried as hard as a kid could to protect them from their father's neglect. And even before their mother deserted them, he would take them out to play or down the road to a pasture to sit when their parents were fighting. But, I think it has affected Jess more than he lets on."

They sipped their tea and gazed out over the pasture in a comfortable silence. Gabi pictured the brothers and her heart broke thinking about them. This ranch was Luke's dream for them. Gabi got it.

"Gabi, Jess likes you. I haven't been around long, but I've seen enough to know when my brother-in-law is interested in a woman."

Gabi's heart stumbled at that. "Oh, I'm sure he's interested in a bunch of them."

"Not that I've seen. Luke wishes there was someone special in his life. And Colt's too, but it will be awhile before Colt has time to think about settling down. He's focused on a World Champion Bull Rider title. So what about you? You seem settled. You have a great career you obviously love. And you are so dedicated and good. I mean, don't think we don't understand what you did. Not everyone would go the extra mile like that. And Susan as well, by sending you out here. That's dedication."

"Thanks." A warm fuzzy feeling enveloped Gabi. Sure, it was nice to know she was appreciated, but she really liked knowing she'd done something to help Montana and her family. "I'm just glad I could help."

But Gabi wondered as Jess and Luke walked

across the yard toward them, could she really help Jess get over his past?

Could she—when she knew she hadn't been completely open about the details of her own?

Chapter Fourteen

"I had a great time tonight, Jess."

He wanted to deny it but it would have been a flat-out lie. Everything in him told Jess to stay away from Gabi, but he was finding that impossible. She'd hit it off with Montana from the moment she'd walked in the door. It was as if the two of them had been friends forever. Luke pumped him for information, when they'd gone out to the barn, wanting to know if there was any progress between them. Progress....

Glancing across the truck cab at Gabi as he drove down the long lane toward the entrance of the ranch, he wasn't ready for the night to end. It was a beautiful full moon and it bathed the pastures in a shimmering, soft light. The moon lilies which dotted the fence line here and there had their white flowers wide open—

"The moon lilies are gorgeous tonight,"

Gabi said, breaking into his thoughts as if reading them.

"You mean my *toxic* jimsonweeds or thornapples," he corrected, calling them by the names she'd used the other day when she'd told him they were toxic.

She chuckled lightly. "Thankfully for you, these cool-looking plants are horrible tasting."

"Lucky for me, or I'd've had to destroy one of my favorite plants to look at in the moonlight." Since the flowering bush only bloomed at night, it made quite a statement when all the white flowers opened up and the moonlight reflected off them. He slowed the truck at the intersection of one of the gravel roads leading toward the north pastures. Ahead of him was the blacktop road leading to Mule Hollow and Gabi's house.

"Do you have to be home right now?"

"No," she said, sitting up expectantly. "What's on your mind?"

"It's too pretty of a night to go home just yet. How about I show you my favorite spot on the ranch?"

Her smile dug in deep. "Hit the gas, dude. I'm game."

Energy zinged through Jess as he changed direction and headed toward his favorite spot.

This was not at all what he'd planned. But he was doing it…

Just being friendly. That was it.

There was nothing romantic about this.

Nothing. Not one thing…

"This is the most *romantic* place I've ever seen." Gabi gasped, in awe. They'd driven up a hill and when they had topped the rise, there was a lake shimmering in the moonlight down the slope on the other side. It was gorgeous.

Jess's eyes inflated at her words.

"Calm down," Gabi said, hiding the fact that her heart was about to thump right out of her chest at the beauty around her—cowboy included. "It's not like you brought me here for anything like that. But it is romantic. You can admit it."

"Sure, whatever," he said. Pushing open his door, he got out and stomped to the front of the truck like he was angry. Gabi followed him, feeling a little wary.

"You did tell me it was your favourite place," she said standing beside him.

He gave her a remorseful smile. "Okay, it is beautiful. Romantic," he said quickly looking away from her. "I think a house would be great here on this spot." Relaxing against the grill of his truck, he took a deep breath. Gabi did too, trying to calm the restless butterflies that once again were in flight. "Can you imagine sitting out here on a back porch every evening, especially on a full moon like tonight with the moonlight shining on the lake like this? Then waking to the sun coming up over that rise every morning?"

Beautiful. "It would be great. You should do that," Gabi said. She could see him here. After the conversation she'd had with Montana, she *wanted* to see him here, happy and content. She was suddenly curious.

"Where do you live now?"

"There's a small house—more like a cabin on the other side of the property. I live there. Colt has a place not too far from me, though he more or less just bunks there since he's gone so much. Luke was going to take one of the smaller houses but we wouldn't hear of it."

"So one day, when you have a family, you should build here."

That got her another odd look.

"I'm not too sure I'll ever have a family. I keep telling Luke he should build here, but he won't. Tells me I need to build on this spot because I like it so much." His words were quiet. They rang through the night like the sound of wind rustling through trees down below them, soft but distinct.

"Why do you always say you won't have a family?" Gabi leaned against the grill beside him. "Does it have to do with your past? If so, then that's a shame."

He crossed his arms and stared sideways at her. "It's not a shame, not if that's the way I want it."

"Nope, it's sad. Why wouldn't you want a family?"

"I have a family," he said, curtly. "I have Luke, Montana and Colt. And I'll have more as they add on."

Why wouldn't Jess want a family of his own? She had to know. And she had to understand it. Her heart ached for him deeper than she could fathom.

"Jess," she said, hesitantly. "You told me your mother ran off and left you with your dad—who was irresponsible and drunk all the time. Are you afraid you might turn out like that?"

"Gabi, I would *never* be like that," he gritted out through stiff jaws, his eyes flashed fireworks. "Why would you say that?"

She hadn't meant to hurt him, but it was clear she had insulted him.

He stared hard at the water down the hill below them. The silence pulsing through the air between them had a life of its own, it was so thick with unspoken words. Gabi kept quiet, giving him time to process what she was trying to say and herself time to figure out why she was pushing this issue.

"I'll be the first to admit that my past plays a huge role in my decision making," he said slowly, thoughtfully. "But it's never been because I'm afraid of being like them." The last word held an edge—a thin, almost unnoticeable edge but it was so sharp it could cut through stone.

"Then what is it?" She just could not let this pass. She felt she was supposed to push this issue. Either that or she was just plain nosy. She'd never thought of herself like that. Bold and open yes, but not nosy. Jess might look at it in a completely different light.

Anger shot across his expression. "What is this—twenty questions?"

Gabi blushed in the moonlight. She pushed away from the truck but didn't move away. "No, but I feel like I'm supposed to push this issue."

"Why would you feel like that?"

"Honestly, Jess, I don't know. I'm asking myself the same question, but I feel it. Frankly, I like you and I'm concerned for you. A nurse at a hospital who didn't know me at all was concerned for me and made a huge difference in my life. I'm a new friend, but maybe pushing this issue will make a difference in yours."

Jess was staring at her like she'd lost her mind. But she couldn't back away from this. It was as if God was telling her to make a move.

"You are a great guy, Jess Holden. I get completely irritated at you sometimes. In the very short time that we've known each other, you've been fairly pushy, thinking your way's the only way. But I know that you've been like that because you were concerned for me. Like a parent who cares would be. You'd make a great daddy. It concerns me that you aren't considering it because of the way your parents acted towards you. Just so you know—you would *never* be like them."

His lips flattened in the firm but cute way they tended to do when he was frustrated. Funny that she knew his expressions so well after such a short time.

"I'm not saying that to pity you. I'm in awe of the way you and Luke have handled your past. And though I haven't met Colt yet, it sounds like he's handled it well, too. It just concerns me that you've closed this door when you are so obviously meant to be a family man."

He was staring at her with eyes that had mellowed as she'd rambled quickly forward with her speech. "I know I'm talking like a crazy woman and I'm expecting you to tell me to button my lip." She smiled at him, feeling her dimple digging into her cheek. "My flappy lips almost have a mind of their own. I'll blame them if you're mad at me."

His brows crinkled more.

"It's true, though, what I'm saying," she continued when he just stared at her with those eyes that reflected the moon on the pond like the teal ocean water they were so similar in color to. That look sent a shiver of awareness coursing over her skin. The man affected her on so many levels she couldn't compute them all.

Gabi refocused on what she'd been saying. "You talk about a house up here on this hill, and you know as well as I do that this hill needs a family to enjoy." She flung her arms open wide. "This would make the perfect patio, for barbecues and fish fries, for hotdog roasts and marshmallow s'mores. You see it, but I get the feeling that because of your past you're afraid to grasp it."

Abruptly, Jess pushed away from the truck and strode to the edge of the hill. "I'm not afraid of being like my parents, Gabi," he whispered gruffly.

He leaned back his head so he was looking straight up at the sky before turning toward her. "Don't you get it? I'm afraid the woman *I marry* will be…that she'll run out on me." He turned away from her again, staring at the lake.

In the darkness a hoot owl let out an eerie call that sent a chill down Gabi's spine. She took a deep breath and closed the distance between them. She lifted her hand and let it hover near his back, uncertain if she should touch him but unable to help herself. Finally, she placed her hand between his shoulder blades. The tension was undeniable, even worse at her touch.

"Why are you doing this?" Jess asked, quietly.

"I understand that fear in a way," Gabi said just as softly. "But sometimes you have to fight the fear by ignoring it." She was trying her hardest to do that herself, she almost said, but couldn't make the words come out. He turned to look down at her. They were so close and Gabi fought against the urge to wrap her arms around him.

"I can't risk it. It wouldn't be fair to the kids."

Gabi's heart pounded, her palms were sweating and she could sure use a whack in the head for how much she wanted to kiss Jess Holden and tell him that there were women out there who would never think of leaving. She topped the list.

His eyes, oh so beautiful and expressive, searched hers. "Kids need security. They need love. I'm an adult now and I got over it. Thankfully I had Luke and Colt. But some don't have that."

He hadn't gotten over it and Gabi knew it. "There is one major element you are missing in this equation, Jess. Your children would have *you* if for some fluke of a reason your wife walked out on you—which I have to say, frankly, would make her the stupidest woman in the world."

The corner of his mouth hitched at that, sending an electrical shock through her. "A little rough there, don't you think?"

"I'll ask God to forgive me. I get a little excitable sometimes. But really, Jess, you know what I mean. You are a great guy, an honorable guy. You came to my rescue twice. You are a hero to strangers. You would be that and more to your family."

"I don't know—"

"Don't you even dare! Without a doubt I know you would give that sort of devotion to someone you loved and were responsible for. No doubt about it. Someone would be less than smart if they walked away from you," she finished, daring him to deny it.

Moments ticked by and the tension straining between them hummed in the night.

"Thanks," he said, finally.

"No thanks needed, it's a fact," she snapped, frustrated by her emotions.

He reached and gently brushed a stray hair out of her eyes, his fingers lingering at her temple, reminding her of that day in the woods. "Your fiancé was a fool for walking away from you."

Gabi's heart ground to a halt like a fifty-car train crashing into a concrete wall. She hadn't forgotten as she was giving her impassioned speech that the man who was supposed to have loved her had walked away without a backward glance.

Jess looked tenderly at her. "I hope it didn't hurt you too deeply. You'll move on to better things."

Suddenly her voice wouldn't come. "Thanks," she managed at last. "For me it was right. God delivered me from the mistake of my life when Phillip walked away. There is no sadness, at least not anymore. Other than regret that I couldn't see how unhealthy my lifestyle was. Or that I was not living in the will of God like that."

"I'm glad you're okay."

"I am so happy and relieved that I'm where

I am today." A twinge of guilt plagued her but her insides were quaking from his nearness and the fact that his hand had trailed from her temple to rest on her shoulder. Its warmth radiated through her. Her gaze drifted to his lips. And any guilt she felt about not opening up more to Jess was overshadowed by this moment.

"That still doesn't change the fact that this guy was a fool." Jess stepped closer—her heart pounded faster. His gaze searched hers as she tore her eyes away from his lips.

You don't want this. The voice inside Gabi's head spoke softly even as she closed her eyes and her heart raced. She hadn't come here tonight to fall for Jess. She'd come here to let God lead her. To help her help him.

Just like in the woods the week before, she couldn't do it. Couldn't let this happen.

"Hang on," she gasped, and stepped back, her mind reeling. She held up a hand and fought for a voice. "Hold on. This is not part of my game plan."

Not part of her game plan? That's what she'd said before she'd practically broken her neck getting away from him.

Jess had lost his mind. He'd almost kissed Gabi when he knew there was no way he wanted to get involved with her. Then she'd gone and said she wasn't interested in getting involved with him. What had he been thinking?

This wasn't the way this evening should have gone. Romance wasn't on either one of their radars and yet the magnetic pull of attraction was as visible as a white horse in the middle of a group of bays.

About halfway to her house, she said, "I like you, Jess. It's nothing against you. I just can't get involved with you. Trust me on that."

He laughed. The woman never ceased to surprise him.

"For years I've been running from the Lord. And now that I've found Him, I feel like I'm catching up. I have so much to do, to learn. I almost made a huge mistake when I planned to marry Phillip. He dumped me as soon as I'd changed my life. But if he hadn't, I had already decided before I told him that I was going to cut my ties and run." She grimaced. "That sounds terrible doesn't it?"

He pulled into town. Everything was locked up tight this late at night. Main Street glowed in the moonlight, leading a lighted path to the small house where Gabi lived beside the huge old family home Adela had turned into a small apartment house.

"You weren't married yet. That's the time to

cut your ties and run. Especially before kids were involved. And if your faith beliefs were a problem that's a big one." He pulled up behind her small car and turned off the ignition. He wasn't ready to drop her off and leave. Not yet.

"What about your faith, Jess? Have you trusted the Lord with your life? You said you're a Christian, but from all accounts you hardly go to church."

"You don't have to go to church to believe."

"True. But you and I both know there's more there than that."

How did she know so much? It was almost like she could read his thoughts. "I've got a few issues."

"Also stemming from your past?"

He cocked his head and met her unwavering gaze. "You don't give up, do you?"

She smiled. "I'm paying you back for being bossy to me a few times."

He chuckled despite the serious conversation. "So is it?"

"Maybe, Gabi. Yes. But it's not something I'm willing to talk about. That's between me and God."

She opened her door and stepped down from the truck. "Then I'll pray for you. At least I can do that."

He followed her to her door. The night was

finally coming to an end and it was almost impossible for him to want to walk away. He liked her open honesty. Her ability to see past him—hard as it was at times, he liked seeing how she thought.

At the door, under the shadow of the porch, with the scent of the jasmine bush that grew at the end of Adela's porch behind the swing, she looked up at him. "It was a great night."

Jess rammed his hands into his pockets of his jeans fighting the need to reach for her. "It was."

Looking at her, unable to stop himself, Jess slid his hands free and moved forward.

One step at a time, slow and easy, Jess moved toward Gabi. His eyes boring into hers in a completely unnerving way.

"This is crazy," she whispered.

His eyes mellowed. "Yeah, it is," he said, even as he slid his hand to cup the back of her neck and gently tugged her toward him.

Gabi's heart floated. His eyes searched hers, darkened and this time she had no will to stop him. Her internal war ceased the instant his lips met hers.

All she thought about was being in Jess's arms. This was nothing like she'd ever experienced before. It was as if she could feel her heart in the kiss....

"Gabi," he whispered, pulling away. "I've tried my hardest not to do that, but it's impossible. I can't get you off my mind no matter how hard I try."

He'd tried *not* to think about her? "Those are words to make a girl's heart go pitter-patter," she said, pulling away and forcing a smile.

"I didn't mean it that way." He looked stunned in the porch light.

"I know what you meant, Jess." She moved away from him, feeling like she needed to run from him and get as far away as possible or risk losing her heart. "I know how you feel about a serious relationship. And about my past. That's why I'm confused here. I'm trying to look at reality here. What do you want with me?"

"I..." he stuttered, apparently at a loss for words.

Gabi forced another smile, though it felt pinched. She had the weirdest pain in her heart. "I shouldn't have let you kiss me, Jess," she said, feeling overwhelmingly sad. "We're good as friends. Let's keep it that way. Okay?" It took everything she had to say the words. Friends did not kiss the way that they had. She'd never had the overwhelming compulsion to throw herself into any other friend's arms.

But friends were exactly where this was going to stay.

Jess closed his eyes, leaned back his head and took a deep breath. His hair curled against his collar and brushed the middle of his ear, begging for her to trace her fingers through it. Begging her to smooth away the sudden strain that was etched in his forehead beneath the shadow of his hat.

"I guess I set myself up for this." His voice was full of regret. "But you're right. This thing between us is…"

"Complicated," she finished for him.

His lip lifted on the right side. "Yeah, complicated."

They stared at each other for a long moment. Gabi wondered if he was thinking about the kiss the way she was.

Because she was still thinking about it.

Still wanting more.

And still as certain as ever that she needed to keep a firm line drawn between them. And hope that he would honor that, too.

"Good night, Jess," she said, and walked inside, shutting the door firmly between them. If she was smart she'd keep it that way.

And she would not think about the way his kiss had made her feel.

Chapter Fifteen

Jess's boots echoed through his house as he entered, slamming the door behind him harder than what he'd meant to do. The wall rattled and he got an instant flashback of his father coming home angry and drunk.

Jess never lost his temper. Halting in the small living room, he carefully set his hat on the wall hook then raked his hands through his hair. Gabi Newberry was making him think about things he didn't want to think about. Things he didn't want to want. Family. Kids. He felt a headache coming on and he never had them.

The phone rang, reminding him that Colt was supposed to be coming home tonight.

Jess immediately glanced at his watch. It was ten-thirty and according to Colt it was going to be midnight before he made it in. Maybe he was tired and needed someone to help keep him awake. Reaching for the phone Jess thought it was perfect timing because talking would not be a problem tonight. He had a lot to get off his chest.

"Hey, buddy, I'm glad you called," he said.

"Is this Jess Holden?"

Jess went still at the sound of the man's voice on the other end of the line. A bad feeling swept over him. "Yes, this is Jess."

"Sir, this is State Trooper Trident with the Texas Department of Public Safety. Are you the brother of Mr. Colt Holden?"

Jess and Luke walked into the Kerrville emergency room. Luke's expression was grim and Jess knew his matched his older brother's. The officer had informed him that Colt was okay but that he'd had a head-on collision with a man who'd been drinking. The collision had knocked Colt's truck into another car—a family of four. Everyone except Colt was dead.

Jess and Luke had barely been able to talk the hundred-mile drive from Mule Hollow to Kerrville. The officer had told them that Colt hadn't been to blame, that the drunk went across the line and hit him. Jess and Luke both knew that wouldn't matter when it came to their little brother knowing he'd wiped out an entire family.

It was too terrible to take in. A family...dead.

The thought made Jess ill. He couldn't imagine how Colt felt. And Luke, ever their protector, looked as bad as Jess. Grim and shaken, all they could think about was getting to Colt.

The hospital was pretty quiet when they walked in and a nurse told them Colt's room number.

Luke led the way down what seemed like an endless hallway. Their boots clicked in unison along the glossy floor.

"He's going to be in bad shape," Luke said, repeating what they already knew.

"Yeah," was all Jess could say. It struck him that the whole way down the hallway he'd been praying. This was his little brother. He was twenty-eight-years-old, with the world at his fingertips, and in the blink of an eye everything had changed.

The doctor had said there was barely a scratch on him other than a cut on his forehead, a bruised chin and chest from the steering wheel and seat belt. But the outer scars didn't matter. Luke and Jess knew as they entered Colt's room that their baby brother's life was never, ever going to be the same.

They all knew how deeply internal scars

went. Jess's felt as if they cut all the way through from one side to the other and yet, he couldn't imagine the guilt, pain and utter sorrow that must be going through Colt's head and heart right now.

Luke tapped on the wide wooden door. There was no answer. The television played low in the background, not loud enough to drown out the knock on the door though.

Looking at each other, Jess and Luke silently agreed, and then entered the dimly lit room.

Colt was sitting in a chair. He was staring straight ahead, not up at the TV hanging on the wall, not out the window. But at the wall.

And he didn't acknowledge them when they walked in.

"Colt, hey, buddy," Jess said, forcing his voice to be strong, not to crack. The last thing Colt needed right now was his big brothers falling apart on him. But looking at the pale, hollow expression on Colt's face ripped Jess to shreds.

"We're here now," Luke said, placing his hand on Colt's shoulder.

As if suddenly realizing they were there, his eyes shifted and focused. "Hey, guys."

His voice was flat, no inflection at all. And though his eyes had focused on them, there was no emotion in their depths. Luke's concerned gaze flickered to Jess then back to Colt. It was obvious he was either drugged or in shock. Since the nurse had told them that he'd been given a low dose of sedative in his IV to help him cope, Jess wanted to say what they were seeing was all medication. But he knew it wasn't.

"How are you, buddy?" he asked, though it was apparent Colt wasn't okay.

Colt's gaze moved over to the television and he watched it for a minute, totally expressionless. "I killed that family," he said, his voice as dead as the family who would forever haunt him.

"It wasn't your fault," Luke and Jess said almost in unison. They both knew that didn't matter—people were dead.

He looked blankly from Luke to Jess. "Get me out of here," he said, flatly. "I want to go home."

The morning after she'd let Jess kiss her—which she knew in her heart was wrong, given her past—she needed coffee. Some of Sam's strong, caustic java. And she needed it desperately.

"He's bad off and gonna need time to get over this," App's loud voice carried across the diner as Gabi entered. Sitting at their usual spot at the front window table, App and Stanley weren't hunched over their checker game as usual. Instead, they were talking, and it appeared every cowboy in the joint was tuned into what they were saying.

"It shor is a shame fer him and that family," Stanley said, looking really sad.

"And the drunk, too," Sam grunted, pausing at the checker table, coffeepot in his hand, he shook his head. Men from all the tables nodded agreement, looked sad then went back to eating with solemn expressions on their faces.

"Hey, Gabi," Sam said. There was no missing the grim set of his lips.

"What's up, Sam?" Gabi asked, concerned. "Did something happen? Y'all look really tore up."

"It's turable. Jest turable," App muttered.

"What?" They were frightening Gabi.

"Colt Holden had an awful wreck last night," Sam told her, shaking his head.

Gabi's heart lurched. "No!"

"He's alive," Stanley offered. "But I know that boy, and this is gonna tear him apart."

Gabi's thoughts flew instantly to Jess. "What happened? How bad was it?"

"Some drunk ran him over and knocked his truck into a family," App scoffed.

"Wiped 'em all out 'cept fer Colt," Sam said,

shaking his head as he headed back toward the kitchen.

"Have Jess and Luke gone to him?"

"Yup," Stanley supplied. "Montana went after thar mother. Didn't want her to find out from strangers."

Gabi could only imagine the anguish Colt was experiencing. He and his brothers had been through so much. How was he handling this? How was Jess handling it?

"Where are they?" she asked, following Sam into the kitchen.

"Kerrville," Sam said, grabbing plates.

She couldn't help herself. She needed to be with Jess.

The strength of her need to be by his side scared her a little, but she paid it no mind in the face of the extreme crisis the Holden family was going through.

She prayed for the lost family and hoped with all her heart that they'd find peace with the Lord. Thinking about the drunk man causing all of this had her flashbacking to what could have been her own experience. Standing in the middle of Sam's kitchen, it hit her suddenly how similar the circumstances were to her own near miss. Only this had no happy ending.

Nauseated, Gabi managed a goodbye and

headed out the rear door of the building. On the back porch of the diner, she bent over and grabbed her knees, sucking in air as she willed the nausea to go away. *God protected me. He sent someone to show me the light at the right moment.* Thankfulness washed over her like nothing she'd ever experienced before. Yes, she'd been thankful in the hospital when she'd realized how close she'd come to disaster but this—oh, what must Colt be going through?

Standing up, Gabi's hand shook as she grabbed the porch railing for support. Stepping down off the elevated porch, she headed toward her car. She had to see Jess, had to see if there was anything at all that she could do to help.

Jess was standing outside the hospital taking a break. Colt was unhooked from the IV and they were waiting on the doctor to come by and release Colt to go home. Montana had arrived with his mother and was with Luke and Colt.

He'd had to come outside for a breather to escape all the overwhelming care and concern oozing from Rhonda. He'd had to get some fresh air.

He hadn't felt this angry in a long time. And there was one thing he knew. He couldn't go back up there right now. Not like this.

Striding off the sidewalk, he headed toward

a distant clump of trees at the far edge of the parking lot. Trees equaled solitude. Even the small clump offered a measure of seclusion—in case someone decided to come looking for him.

He couldn't take his mother right now, inside or out here.

At the moment he didn't care to be found by anyone. He had to get his head on straight so he could be of use to Colt.

He made it to the trees and walked to the back side of them. There was a fence there and then a vacant lot. Jess was relieved. Grasping the top of the chain link fence, he stared at nothing, dropped his head back and looked up accusingly.

"What is it with You?" he growled. "I just don't get it."

"Jess?"

He flinched at Gabi's soft voice. Spinning around, he found her standing at the edge of the trees. She was breathing hard, as if she'd run across the parking lot after him. She had a stricken expression. He'd never been more happy to see anyone in all of his life. In two strides he met her, wrapped his arms around her and buried his face in her soft, scented hair.

Thank You, God. He closed his eyes and held her.

"I got here as soon as I could," she whispered, clutching him close.

Nearly breaking her in half, Jess hung tight, and yet he couldn't bring himself to loosen his hold. "Thank you" was all he could manage to say for the first few moments.

Nodding, Gabi gently continued to hold onto him as if willing strength and emotion and support to him.

In all of his life Jess had never felt like this. It was as if Gabi filled a hole that had been empty forever.

"How is Colt?" she asked at last, rubbing her hand along his back, gently easing the impossible tension knotted there.

Pulling away but still holding on to her, he drank her in. "I can't believe you came."

"I couldn't get here fast enough."

He took a deep breath trying to process his emotions. "He's not saying much. I think he's in shock. When we first got here, he was medicated and kind of stunned. But now there's no meds in him and he still seems in his own world. It's hard to explain. It's killing him. That's what it's doing."

"Oh, Jess." Gabi's eyes filled with tears.

"A well-meaning little lady came by with books and magazines about seven this morning and there was a picture of the family and the drunk on the front page."

Gabi gasped. "Oh, no! Did he see it?"

"We all did," he said, quietly, rubbing his forehead. "Colt's been more withdrawn ever since. He's refusing to say anything. Just staring out the window like he's the one that's dead."

Tears filled Gabi's eyes. "Is there anything I can do?"

Jess stared at her, loosening his grip on her so she could breathe. "I'm not sure at this moment there's anything any of us can do. If it were me in Colt's shoes, I'd just want to be alone. I'd *need* to be alone. Right now he's got Luke and Montana looking after him. My mother is up there, too." He added the last sentence with total lack of emotion.

Gabi remembered their conversation and knew this was hard for him on so many levels.

"My brother is hurting and I'm down here because I can't stand to be in the same room with her. Luke has forgiven her. And Colt has too, in his own way."

Gabi didn't know what to do to ease his pain as he wrapped his hands again around the chain link fence.

"What you're feeling is understandable," she said quietly. "Totally understandable."

He stared at her. "You think so?"

Anger for him flashed in her eyes. "Sure. Look at what she did to y'all. Forgiving her for that would be unbelievably hard. Yes, we're supposed to, but that doesn't make it easy."

He wasn't sure what he'd expected but it wasn't this—especially the fire attached to her words.

She must have realized that she'd shocked him because she huffed out a sigh and her shoulders slumped slightly.

"I know, I know. As a Christian, I'm a little confused about my feelings toward your mother." She frowned, looking frustrated. Despite everything that was going on, Jess wanted to smile.

"You're not alone. That's how I feel every day," he said, acknowledging a connection between them. Just her being here, beside him, lifted his spirits. "Right now this is not about me, it's about Colt, and I need to be there for him. Will you come up with me?"

Gabi reached for his hand. "That's why I came."

Gabi and Jess didn't make it upstairs. Instead they met Jess's family coming around the corner. Colt was in a wheelchair with a nurse guiding him out the door.

Gabi's first thought was that Colt looked lost. As if he didn't know what to do from here on out. She considered that, and realized if something as tragic as this had happened to her, she would feel the same.

Introductions were made between Gabi, Colt and Rhonda. Gabi felt a little awkward, what with Colt being in such a state of shock. It was apparent that he wasn't in a speaking mood but, as if on autopilot, he nodded at her and even gave a distant smile. Rhonda, a thin woman with the same sandy-brown hair and coffee-colored eyes as Colt, looked nervous and worried. Gabi guessed her to be in her late forties or very early fifties. Which would have made her fairly young when the boys were little. She held out her hand and Gabi took it. It was icy cold, but her grip was firm, as if she were hanging on for assurance.

"I'll get the truck," Luke said, after he'd made the introductions.

"I can walk," Colt insisted, pushing up from the wheelchair.

The nurse laid her hand on his shoulder. "I'm sorry, Colt, but you have to wait until the vehicle is here and then you can get up."

For the first time since Gabi met him, emotion sparked across his face. "I'm *not* injured," he growled.

"I know," the nurse said kindly. "It's procedure. If I let you up and that security camera there catches me, then my job is on the line."

"Just a little longer, honey," Rhonda said, patting his shoulder.

Gabi caught Jess's flinch at the exchange.

Feeling like an intruder into a family affair, Gabi waited to the side as Colt climbed into the truck. Jess looked at her and then the truck and she realized he was torn on which vehicle to ride in.

"Don't worry about me. You go with your brothers." She gave him a smile. "I only came to show my support."

"Are you sure? You drove all this way and now you'll have to ride back alone."

"I'm fine, Jess. Go." Touched that he was thinking of her. To him alone she said, "You need to be in there with Colt. Just the three of you. A car and a long drive make the perfect place for good conversations. You don't owe me anything for coming."

He gave a curt nod, squeezed her hand then strode over and climbed into the backseat of the four-door truck.

Watching them pull away from the curb, Gabi said a prayer that the next hundred miles to Mule Hollow would be miles toward healing for Colt. Turning, she met Rhonda's curious eyes.

It struck her that Jess's road to healing was up against a brick wall with nowhere to go. And she hadn't helped his situation one bit.

"Thank you," Rhonda said, her voice heavy with emotion.

"Yes," Montana added. "Jess seemed better after you came. He was so tense that we were worried about him."

Guiltily, Gabi's gaze flicked to Rhonda. If she knew why his nerves were better, Rhonda would feel like dirt.

Gabi gave Montana a smile and tried to include Rhonda, though her eyes didn't meet the older woman's. "I'm glad. I didn't know what else I could do. But I had to come."

Gabi thought about that statement all the way home.

I had to come....

She had known Jess Holden for less than a month and she felt so connected to him that she'd *had* to be there for him.

She knew she was kidding herself if she dismissed it as simply being a good Christian girl.

Jess Holden had a hold on her that was like nothing she'd ever felt before. And there was just no getting by the fact.

Chapter Sixteen

When Gabi arrived at the clinic later that Monday, she found Susan in the rear grinding down an old horse's back teeth. Like the human nose, a horse's teeth never stopped growing—unlike a nose they had to be buffed down every once in a while.

"You made good time. How is he?" Susan asked, pulling the foot-long dental tool from the horse's mouth.

Gabi had headed straight for the clinic as soon as she'd gotten into town. Susan had been nice enough to let her take off a few hours so she could drive to Kerrville and she wanted to make sure to show her appreciation by returning to work as quickly as possible. Besides that—she needed to be busy.

"He's struggling," she said. "As you can imagine, he's sad. In shock. Distant."

"That's what I was afraid of," Susan said. "How were Luke and Jess holding up?"

"They're very worried about him. This was my first time to meet Colt and he was really quiet. I only saw him for a minute. Jess was out front when I got there and I spent time talking with him. He's pretty shook up himself."

Susan crossed her arms, compassion in her expression. "I can see where Jess and Luke would be torn up over this. My Cole lost his first wife tragically young and he was having a hard time with it when I came along. His brothers were extremely worried for him. The Turner men feel each other's pain…I'm sure the Holden men are no different."

Gabi's heart ached. "They're close. Especially since they relied so heavily on each other growing up."

"True. In a way so did Cole and his brothers. Except they were teenagers when their parents died in a plane crash. Jess, Luke and Colt were really young when their parents skipped out emotionally and physically on them."

"What do you make of their situation? Their mother was at the hospital."

"I think it's a tough situation. She lives in Fredericksburg from what I've been told. That's not too far from Kerrville. I wonder if Colt was trying to make it to her house last night."

"I don't think so."

"I really do think a mother, who walked out on you young and now wants back in after you're all grown up and don't need her any more, would be hard to deal with. It's sad. But from what I understand, Luke has asked her many times to move out to the ranch, but she won't do it. God can heal all wounds…in His time and given the opportunity."

Gabi believed that, but the hurts ran deep. "Jess has a hard time with it." She couldn't go into detail since she was privy to Jess's thoughts on the subject, and it felt far too personal to reveal his emotions.

"Understandable. Maybe that's why she hasn't taken Luke up on his offer."

"Maybe." Gabi tapped her boot on the floor impatiently. "You know, Susan. It just really makes me angry."

Susan was smiling at her. "Yeah, it would. That too is very understandable."

That struck Gabi as odd. "Why do you say it like that?"

Susan gave a knowing smile. "When you care for someone, you don't want to see them hurting. It's as simple as that."

Gabi's mouth fell open. "I can sure tell you one thing. There is nothing simple about it! Not one, single, complicated thing."

* * *

Jess and Luke watched as Colt paced across his small cabin's front porch. Inside Montana and his mother were putting up the groceries they'd bought for him. Rhonda had insisted on mixing up a casserole for him—though he'd said he didn't want anything. Jess thought it was pretty sad that after all the times as little kids they'd gone to bed hungry or after eating a peanut butter sandwich, provided by Luke, that now their mother wanted to cook.

Resentment warred inside him but he pushed the feelings aside and focused on Colt. Jess and Luke had tried to talk to him all the way home from the hospital. They'd given him ample opportunity to open up to them, but Colt had remained quiet. The drive had seemed endless.

Jess wasn't used to being out of control and lately it was happening a lot. With the cattle dying and this thing going on between him and Gabi…and now Colt's situation.

Things like the issues between him and his mom. He knew how he felt and how he was going to react. Watching Colt, he didn't know how Colt felt, and there was nothing Jess could do to figure it out unless Colt opened up.

"Okay, we're all set inside," Rhonda said, coming out onto the porch.

Montana followed and went over to Colt. "You should be good for a few days."

"Maybe you should take a little time off from the circuit," Rhonda added. "Get this behind you."

Colt stiffened. "Thanks for your help," he said, almost too politely. "I need to talk to Jess and Luke alone now."

Rhonda looked stricken. "Sure, we'll just go inside—"

"I mean *alone*." His eyes, as dead as they'd been all day, darkened with even more shadows when he looked solemnly up at Montana.

Montana nodded in understanding. "Rhonda and I will go to our house. You just call us if you need anything."

Rhonda obviously got it too, and didn't argue anymore. Instead, looking beat down she followed Montana off the porch and out to her parked truck. Within minutes the three brothers were alone.

Colt raked his hands through his hair, then closed his eyes and leaned his head back. He looked as if he'd aged ten years overnight.

"I can't stay here." His words were firm, his eyes still shut. "If I stay here, I'll go crazy with my thoughts." He looked at them then.

"You need to take it easy—"

"*No,* Luke," he snapped, storming to the edge of the porch and swinging around. "Don't y'all get it? I killed those people. *Me. My* truck. Wiped them out in one fell swoop. How am I ever gonna live with that?"

His words were so broken and anguish-filled that Jess felt the sting of hot tears well up in his eyes.

"It wasn't your fault," Jess tried, though he knew if he were in Colt's shoes, it wouldn't stop the nightmare.

"God's not going to hold you accountable for that, Colt. You'll have to let it go." Luke's words were as gruff and full of emotion as Jess's.

"Don't you get it, I hold myself accountable. I was almost asleep at the wheel when that thoughtless drunk hit me head-on. If I'd have just pulled over half a mile back, they'd all still be alive."

"Maybe, maybe not," Luke said. "Only God knows that, Colt. You can't think that way."

Colt's grief-stricken eyes slammed them. "I can't think any other way. There were two little kids and a mom and dad in that car going on vacation. God—" Two strides and he sank into a chair and dropped his head into his hands.

Jess felt the sting of tears again. He hadn't

cried since he was a little kid—hadn't known he still could. But this was tearing him up inside.

Luke stepped forward. "I know you don't understand this. We don't either, but the Bible tells us to trust in the Lord with all our hearts and lean not unto our own understanding," Luke continued, trying to talk to him but Colt just shook his head at the scripture.

"Understanding," he growled, springing up from his seat. "How am I supposed to understand this? If I'd been alert, this never would have happened. They'd be alive and that drunk would have awakened the next morning blissfully unaware of what he'd almost done the night before." He rubbed his forehead with one hand, the back of his neck with the other. He seemed almost wild with grief.

"I need a truck," he said after a second. "I'm hitting the road. I've got rodeos to get to and rides to make."

His truck had been destroyed, and for the first time it registered to Jess that he was without a way to get around. Jess had left his truck here at Colt's house before going to the hospital. Now, realizing the truth of what Colt was saying, he knew sitting here in the middle of the woods with nothing but the nightmare of what had happened haunting him wouldn't be good for his little brother. Without hesitating, Jess reached in his pocket and pulled out his keys.

"Here, it's yours," he said, moving to drop them into Colt's outstretched palm. "I'll drive my Chevy around town. You do what you need to do, brother."

His eyes hard with emotion, Luke stepped up, grabbed Colt in a bear hug. His hands were white their grip was so strong. "We're here if you need us." He stepped back, his voice nearly breaking before he took control and his eyes glittered. "But don't do anything stupid. And call us. I wish you'd stay, but I get it."

Jess grabbed him in a quick embrace then, emotion clogging his throat. His gut told him this was what Colt needed to do but he couldn't stand the thought of watching him drive away. "Are you sure?" he asked. "Maybe you need to see a counselor or someone?"

Colt shook his head. "I don't know what I need, I just don't know." He strode inside and they followed him into his bedroom. Grabbing a bag out of the closet, Colt started yanking clothes off the racks. His other bags had been destroyed in the wreck. Jess and Luke had taken a change of clothes for him to the hospital when they'd gone. He paused after stuffing socks into the bag and zipping it up. "It should have been me. Why couldn't I have been the one killed?"

"Come on, Colt," Luke said. "It wasn't meant to be."

Colt's eyes flashed hard and cold. "Yeah." He strode past them and headed to the door, anger and emotion blowing up as he hit the screen with the back of his hand. They followed him. All he had to show from a crash where his truck had turned into a crumpled piece of sheet metal was a cut on his forehead and a slight limp from his bruised hip that they hadn't realized he had until this morning. All in all, it wasn't much physically. What was inside of him was enormous, and Jess was afraid, potentially destructive.

"God had His hand on you in that wreck," Luke said, his arms crossed. "Don't forget that, Colt."

Even Jess had to admit that no way had Colt come out of the wreck without God's protection.

"Yeah." Colt tossed the bag in the back of Jess's truck and tore open the door. "I'd have rather He'd had it on that family."

"Colt, don't talk that way." Luke moved forward, but Colt was already in the truck, cranking the key. The look on his face was a mixture of grief and anger.

Anger so fierce it had Luke and Jess both stopping in their tracks as Colt spun tires and headed out the drive.

Chapter Seventeen

It was driving Gabi crazy not to go and see Jess. She'd worked the rest of the afternoon with Susan and then come home to her house and paced the floor for an hour. She'd taken a long hot shower, and after that she'd cleaned out her refrigerator. She was taking the trash out to the alley when headlights alerted her that someone had just pulled into her driveway. Her heart leaped at the possibility that it might be Jess.

She knew what Susan had said was true. She cared for Jess. Thinking about him now had her wanting to throw herself into his arms and tell him he wasn't alone in this, that she was there for him.

It confused her but that was just the way it was. Complicated.

He was standing on her front porch when she

rounded the corner. "Hey." She paused going up on the second step. "I hoped it was you. How are you? How is Colt?"

He lifted the plastic bag in his hand. "I brought ice cream."

His avoiding her question told her everything wasn't okay. Of course she hadn't expected it to be.

"I was having such a craving for ice cream. How did you know?" she said, in an upbeat tone. Maybe what he needed was some sunshine on a dark day. That she could give him.

Walking up the steps she opened the door. "Come on in. What kind did you bring?"

"You know I had to drive all the way out to the highway to get this, and their selection isn't the best. Will chocolate chip do?"

"My favorite! How did you know?"

He chuckled. "I'm talented that way. I bet you didn't guess that about me did you?"

She led the way into the kitchen and took two bowls from the cabinet. "I had a feeling the first time you threw me over your shoulder that you were a man of many talents. So I'm not surprised that you read my thoughts and knew chocolate chip was my favorite."

He pulled the carton from the bag. It was the familiar yellow tub with a gold rim.

"*Blue Bell!* Now we're talking some serious 'like' here."

"Texas ice cream is the only way to go."

Gabi played along with him, smiling when she could see in his eyes that he had things to say, now just wasn't the time. Maybe he just needed a breather. Whatever was going on, she went with him. She pulled an ice cream scoop from the drawer and held it up. "This belonged to my great granddad. It came from an original soda shop that used to be here in town."

"Cool."

"Mmm-hmm," she murmured, digging into the softened ice cream. Mule Hollow didn't actually have a grocery store. It had been so small that it couldn't support a grocery anymore and the family-owned one that had been here closed up several years earlier. The convenience store on the highway was over fifteen miles away. Everyone had to travel the seventy miles to Ranger, which was the nearest town of any size, to do real grocery shopping.

Jess was studying pictures on the wall behind the kitchen table. There was a formal dining room on the other side of the wall but most of the meals that Gabi remembered the best had been eaten at the oak table here in the kitchen. The pictures were the same now as had been there her whole life.

"Who are all of these people?"

She carried the bowls of ice cream to the table. "That darling little gal in the red cowgirl outfit is the one and only me. I'm a cute little rascal, aren't I?"

"No kidding? That's really you?"

"What, you didn't think I could be so cute? I'm hurt."

"Funny girl. You are one cute four-year-old… that is about how old you are, isn't it?"

"I sure am," Gabi said, then pointed at the picture beside hers. "And that one there is my mom and Gram with my grandpa. And that one there of the pretty young woman and the two men, well that's my grandpa, my Gram and Sam. They were all best friends growing up here in Mule Hollow."

"*Wow,* look how young they are."

Gabi smiled. She loved the pictures. "Sam has always been there for my Gram. He's a stand-up guy."

"Yeah, everyone around here could always tell he cared for Miss Adela. All those years after your granddad died, he never exactly made his move. He just was—"

"Devoted to her," Gabi finished, then she sighed. "I've always wondered what a love like that would feel like. It's special. Of course my Gram is special. I can totally understand someone loving her that much."

Jess turned and stared at her. "You're just as deserving of love like that, too."

She laughed at that. "Believe me, I'm nowhere near the woman my Gram is. I can be downright hard to love at times and I know it."

Jess lifted his hand, hesitated for a second and then touched her cheek with his fingertips. "I think you're pretty lovable."

Gabi liked it. She liked the look in his eyes and the touch of his fingertips. She liked the sincerity and tone of his voice.

She couldn't breathe. She longed for his kiss again. And yes, that kiss had been on her mind all afternoon, hidden under layers of concern for his brother. And worry for Jess. Unable to stop herself she stepped closer to him and his hand slipped beneath her hair and cupped the back of her neck as he'd done earlier. The simple touch had her head spinning. All good intentions evaporated. He needed her.

"How are you?" she asked, softly letting her fingertips curl against his jaw before she let them slip behind his neck and lace together.

His gaze melded into sadness before he closed them completely. "He left. He told us he couldn't take sitting around with nothing but the nightmare of what had happened haunting him. I gave him my truck to use." He looked at her now, pulled her close and rested his temple against her hair. "I didn't know what else to do for him."

Gabi held onto Jess, feeling his pain. "Do you think he'll be okay? I mean, how was his state of mind?"

Jess was quiet for moment, Gabi could feel his back muscles tense. "He was mad. Angry. Angry that if someone had to die, why couldn't it have been him instead of that poor family."

"Wow. That's tough."

Jess nodded against her hair. "Rips me up inside."

"Yeah, how could it not?"

Jess moved away from her suddenly, paced across the room and stared out into the backyard. The ice cream sat melting in the bowls, all but forgotten.

"I just don't get God. I really don't, Gabi." He spun on his boot heel and stared at her. Anger boiled from every pore. "I know you can't understand why I'm not all into church and praising God like you are. But I have to tell you, up to this point, I've had a real hard time understanding what He has had against me and my brothers. This seals the deal. I've got no problem believing in God. No problem believing He holds my life in the palm of His hand. Because, believe me, I feel Him yanking my chain every day. This thing with Colt, it tramples me. *I just don't get it.*"

Gabi's hand had gone to her throat in shock by the vehemence of his words and the rage in him.

"Colt had his life headed in a good direction. That family had their whole life ahead of them." He turned his back to her again, slapped a hand to the window frame and leaned hard, his head hanging as he stared at his boots. "Why couldn't God just leave well enough alone? Was happiness for this family too much to ask for? Does Luke need to be looking over his shoulder now, since he's happy?"

Gabi had wanted to do something for the Lord. She never guessed it would be this complicated. This dire. And she knew more clearly than anything that she wasn't up for this task. Half the questions he was asking, she would have also wanted to know the answers. That was one reason this would take someone far more knowledgeable than her. Someone more grounded in the Word.

Someone more qualified.

Like Gram.

Or Sheriff Brady who taught the singles Bible study class on Sunday mornings.

Or the cowboy preacher Chance Turner.

This was way over her head.

Anyone God, but me. Please send the right person!

She stood frozen to the kitchen floor looking at Jess's back. Words stuck in her throat. Any confidence that she could be the go-to person for someone in need went straight out the window. Who did she think she was? She hadn't been studying her Bible anywhere near long enough. God couldn't use her. She might say the wrong thing and totally mess up any hope of helping Jess.

But you have to say something.

Her chest was heaving up and down and her blood was humming with fear. She couldn't do this. *Please, God, send someone else,* she prayed.

But there was no one else but her.

"Jess," she said, breathless with nerves. "Do you think God is picking on you?"

Jess cut his eyes to her. "That sounds pretty childish," he said. "But yeah, in some ways, I do. I know we aren't the only ones out there with a jerk for a father and a selfish mother. I know I'm a grown man and should just get over it. But I'm having a hard time doing that. Honestly, after you came along, I was considering that I might be taking it over the edge and needed to reconsider. But seeing the pain Colt's going through, not a chance."

Gabi was speechless. Actually there was a lot she wanted to say but it was better left unsaid. His words had her angry with him. And disappointed in him, too. He was a stand-up guy. She expected more from him.

Picking up her ice cream, she walked over and dumped it in the sink. No way could she eat it now. Fingers trembling she washed the bowl, feeling queasy. Jess remained at the window as if stuck there.

His attitude irritated her most, like a burr in her saddle. She leaned against the sink and crossed her arms. "You know what I think? I believe what you need to do is get down on your knees and ask God to forgive you."

His head jerked back. "*Him* forgive *me?*"

"Yes. For all this bitterness you have built up inside you. I really, really don't know what I'm doing here, but I just feel like you've got it all wrong. I'm your friend. If I didn't point this out to you, I don't think I would be much of a friend. Jess, I care for you…" she added, knowing she'd gone way past friendship. She'd crossed over into wishing they had something more between them.

"I didn't come here to fight."

She put her hand on her hip. "I know you

didn't. But Jess, Colt's life has changed forever, and I don't know how he's going to deal with this. With God's help, he will be able to. I had—*have*—issues," she corrected, guilt niggling at her. "And God is helping me deal with them. You have issues too, Jess. And you are trying to deal with them on your own. Blaming God instead of asking Him to help you. I think you'd feel so much better if you'd change that."

"Right now, that's not going to happen."

She shook her head. "Stubborn man." She poked him in the chest, leaned in and kissed him on the lips. "You make me crazy." She told herself now was not the time to tell him all of her ugly past. But she promised herself that she would do it soon. Even knowing what it could do to their relationship.

He chuckled. It was a lovely, lovely sound and gave her hope that he would pull out of all of this. And that was what was important.

"You know," she said, "when I first met you, I'd have never known you housed so much anger inside of you. You really mislead me with your upbeat attitude."

"I decided a long time ago not to let my past take over my life. I get tied in knots sometimes, and angry when I think about it. But I'm not going to let it take over. I give my anger air sometimes, let it out of its box, but

I'm never giving it an open gate. You know what I mean?"

"See that's the difference in you and me. I'd have a hard time doing that. When I'm mad, I'm mad. I get over it and don't hold a grudge. You don't let it rule your life but you hold a grudge that runs deep."

"I'm not sure I call it a grudge."

"Then what *do* you call it?"

"Gabi, this is between me and God."

Before she opened her big mouth again and messed up really bad, she remembered that she wanted to help Jess. Not make him so angry he shut her out.

"Okay. Then I guess I'll just pray that the two of you get it straight at some point."

His brows dipped. "You're mad, aren't you?"

She didn't want to lie. "I'm…" She tossed ideas around like marbles in a grinder. "I'm *concerned* but butting out. And you're lucky because before, I'd have given you a very, very hard time."

He smiled and it made her heart glad. There were issues to figure out, but not tonight. Tonight he needed to relax.

"Yeah," he said, relief vibrating in his voice. "Maybe if I do that tonight, I'll think clearer tomorrow."

Gabi fought the urge to move into the shelter

of his arms. Maybe tomorrow she would think clearer too…She was going to pray hard and heavy tonight for that to be the case.

Because she had a feeling she was heading down a one-way street to disaster where Jess Holden was concerned.

Despite that, Gabi understood that she'd crossed a line of no return. She loved Jess Holden.

She loved him.

And when all this was said and done—when he knew the whole dirty truth about her drinking—it was probable that he wouldn't be able to handle it.

But there was time to worry about that later. Tonight Jess needed her.

Reaching for his hand, she smiled. "Come outside with me. I want to show you something."

Chapter Eighteen

Jess's mother was waiting at the ranch office on Saturday morning.

In the past he'd been able to treat her civilly because that was what Luke wanted. Luke wanted him to love her and forgive her, but it seemed an impossible task for Jess. He admitted that he wasn't the man Luke was. Luke had chosen to forgive the inexcusable.

Gabi had asked him that Monday night if he thought God was picking on him. He hadn't expected that.

But then when did Gabi not surprise him?

Still, it had shaken him up a little. He'd already been messed up worrying about Colt, but suddenly Gabi had him wondering about himself as a man.

Here he was, the guy who'd begun to make rescuing her a part-time job. She'd called him a hero in one breath but in another, she asked him if he thought God was picking on him.

She pictured him as some kind of victim.

That didn't sit well at all.

Matter-of-fact it stuck in his gut like he'd swallowed a prickly pear cactus.

After delivering her unforeseen question, she'd stunned him more by taking him outside to sit on her back deck. Gabi told him when they got out there, that before becoming a Christian she'd thought she always needed to be doing something. That she always needed someplace to go, something to fill the silence.

Since giving her life to Christ she'd learned that finding quiet time was essential. She'd asked him not to speak when they went out onto the porch. Just to sit, look up at God's sky and stars and let God spend time with him.

God spend time with *him*. Even though she knew he was struggling with all that had happened in his life and with what had just happened with Colt, she'd asked him to humor her. To do this for her.

He'd been compelled by that. Partly because he was thrown off guard by her very unflattering view of him. And partly because he knew he needed answers. This standoff that he'd been having with God was at its limits.

When he'd finally risen to leave he'd not gotten any answers—but Gabi hadn't asked him questions.

Halfway home he'd realized that he felt more at peace.

And he wanted to see Gabi again.

When she'd shown up at the hospital, he'd never felt like that before nor been so happy to see anyone.

She'd come for him.

To give him comfort. To hold him. To be there for him in a time of need. *His* need.

Through all the anger that had driven Colt away and driven Jess to seek out Gabi at her home last Monday night, he'd almost let all the anger bury her actions. But on the deck in the silence her goodness filtered through the darkness and filled him with peace. Had God sent her to him?

At some point sitting under the stars with her, she'd held out her hand to him again. Just held it out between them. She hadn't looked at him, hadn't said anything, she'd simply—with her head leaned back on the chaise lounge and her eyes on God's sky, as she'd called it—she'd reached out for his hand.

And he'd reached out for hers.

And Jess knew in that moment that Gabi Newberry had changed something inside of him.

Now, looking at his mother, Jess forced himself to walk toward her.

He'd told her they would talk today and he wasn't one to back down from a promise. He'd learned that from Luke.

"Rhonda," he said, unable to call her Mom. "How are you holding up?" She looked drawn and nervous. Something inside him felt some measure of sympathy.

"I'm fine. Worried about Colt, but I'm fine. Thanks for speaking to me. I k-know—" tears swelled in her eyes. "I know it isn't easy for you."

Jess couldn't say anything good so he said nothing at all and willed her not to cry. He fought off the sympathy as she dabbed at her eyes.

"I wanted to talk to you and say again, how sorry I am for running out on you and your brothers. I could give excuses of being young and stressed but that doesn't help, does it?"

No, it didn't help that ten-year-old kid who'd needed her. And he wished it didn't still affect the thirty-year-old man he'd become.

"Nothing I can do will make up for the fact that I did it. I was supposed to have been there for you and your brothers. And for your dad. And I wasn't."

"You don't owe anything to Dad," Jess bit out

vehemently, struck wrong that she would think that. "He wronged you, too. And I get that."

She looked down. "What you don't get is how I turned around and wronged you, too."

Jess nodded. She'd nailed it.

"I honestly can't answer that. I can't get back yesterday no matter how much I want to. But I've been waiting and praying that you could forgive me. That you could give me a second chance even though it's the last thing I deserve. Jess, I'm hoping you can do that. I'm not asking for you to embrace me or anything. I'm just asking for you to let the past go. I'm so proud of the men you boys have become and so ashamed that I had nothing to do with that. But I want to know that you're okay. Can you forgive me?"

Jess realized in that instant that *he* had the choice to make this time. "I'm okay. It'll be all right." Looking at his mother, he knew he wanted to let go of the past. He could do this. After all, like Luke and Colt had both said, she'd been wronged too by the man who was supposed to take care of her.

It was time for Jess to act like a man.

Monday morning Jess and Luke met early to feed the cattle. It had been a long time since they'd had to put this much hay out during the summer. But there wasn't much grass and if there wasn't real rain soon, then by the end of August, there would be no water in most ponds and no grass at all in the grazing lands.

"If this keeps up, we're going to have to sell off the herd," Luke said as they drove to unload the round bale of hay.

They'd already talked about Colt and they understood that burying himself in his bull riding was probably the only way he could deal with the emotions tearing him up right now. Though he hadn't phoned, Luke had called a fellow bull rider who was a friend of theirs. They knew Colt had won the Mesquite Professional Bull Riders event the night before and that he'd drawn one of the meanest bulls out there to ride.

But today they had cattle to feed and a ranch to tend to before Mother Nature did too much damage.

"We've got the stream that's still flowing and a few ponds that aren't dried up yet, so we can hang on for another month before we make that decision." Luke was pushing limits and he and Jess both knew it.

But Jess agreed with him. It had been almost two weeks since they'd found any new dead cattle. The lab results were going to start coming in this week and they'd know something.

Maybe the dead heifers were a fluke of some sort, since no other unexplained deaths had been discovered across the county.

Then they topped the hill and rounded a bend on the other side of woods and Jess spotted it. Another dead animal.

Susan and Gabi both arrived at the ranch not long after Luke had called in the death and they'd made short order of getting the necropsy done.

"Results of some of the earliest plant testing should start trickling in," Susan told them. "Maybe this death will tell us more than the others have."

They discussed every possibility and Jess noticed as they talked that Gabi seemed distracted with the woods. "This section of woods cuts through the pastures where this animal was found and the pasture where the first heifers were discovered. Right?"

"Yeah, that's right," Jess said, walking to stand beside her. Dressed in her usual tank top and jeans, smelling like an apple, Jess was happy to see her. He'd booked to ship a load of cattle on Sunday, and therefore hadn't seen Gabi since he'd left her on the porch two nights before. His day, as bad as it was starting out, brightened the instant she'd driven up with her sunny smile and sweet disposition.

"What are you thinking, Gabi?"

She headed toward her truck. "It's in those woods. I feel it. I've missed something."

Jess followed her to her truck as did Luke and Susan.

"I'm heading back to the office and going to get busy on this," Susan said. "Let me know what you find, Gabi." She grinned at Jess. "She's like a hound dog on a trail. She is not going to give up."

"We figured that out," Luke said, checking his watch. "Jess, do you have this?"

"Sure. You go do what you need to do."

Gabi was gathering up her backpack with her supplies in it. "I'll call the minute we find something, Susan."

There was a pep in her stride and a stiffness in her jaw as she said a quick goodbye and headed toward the woods. Jess didn't waste any time lingering behind.

Gabi concentrated on the ground as she entered the woods. They should have some answers this week coming from the lab but her instinct told her these woods were the key. Sure, there could be a problem with the different plants on the ranch but this was where the real problem existed. The first dead animals had been found across the woods in the other pasture. These woods were where she'd started her search but they were big and maybe she'd missed something.

Jess followed her and she was so glad to see that he seemed better than he had on Saturday. She'd been praying for him and keeping her distance. She'd fallen in love with the cowboy and that tore her up in so many ways. Wasn't being in love supposed to be a joyous, wonderful thing?

Normally. But she knew she'd just set herself up for heartache loving Jess. She also knew she had to tell him the truth. The whole truth.

But first she was going to find what was killing his cattle.

"Is there anything particular we're looking for?" Jess asked, trailing her close.

"Hoof prints. I think there's something somewhere in here that draws them. And it's very deadly." She paused, turning to face him, steeling herself against the emotions that pulled at her. "I think every heifer that finds whatever it is drops dead soon after."

Jess's gaze was unnerving. A gentle smile

curved his lips. "You are one tenacious go-get-
ter—as App would say."

She smiled, feeling happy in the glow of his
admiration. "I like to think so. Keeping busy
keeps me out of trouble."

"You and everyone else."

"Some of us need to stay busy more than
others," she said, heading out again. There was
no better time then now for being busy to keep
her out of trouble. Standing around staring at
Jess was asking for trouble.

Something was wrong with Gabi. He realized it soon after they were in the woods. She'd
pulled back from him. She was here working
and there was a sense of excitement humming
between them because he agreed with her and
thought their killer plant was somewhere in
these woods. It made sense.

But his mind wasn't on the plants. It was on
Gabi.

"Your cattle have totally been coming this
way. Look at this." Gabi waved him over to
where she'd bent down to study a faint cow trail
among the dry underbrush.

Excitement rose in her voice as he looked over
her shoulder. A dangerous thing to do given
that he had pretty much become a huge fan of
apples. He inhaled and his pulse quickened.

She looked over her shoulder and smiled. "Let's see where this leads. You with me?"

"Gabi, I'm with you anywhere you want to go."

She laughed, and he didn't miss the nervous tremor of that laugh.

"Are you okay?" he asked after they'd gone a long way and she'd remained silent. He couldn't ignore his instincts any longer. After how close they'd been on Saturday night, to be treated almost like a stranger felt completely wrong.

Gabi stopped but didn't turn around immediately.

"What's up, Gabi? What's wrong?"

"Careless Weed!" She spun around and stared at him. "Come look, Jess." His instinct told him something was wrong, but he crossed to where she stood, pointing at a common Careless Weed plant. "These are growing all through here," she said pointing to the area ahead of them. The trees had suddenly given way to a tiny meadow and the scraggly weed could be seen everywhere in the dappled sunlight.

"Well, I'll be. Cattle love them," he added, thinking hard. Unlike vetch he knew Careless Weed was toxic to cattle. But only if eaten in large amounts and without other food sources. A rancher knew to watch out for patches of them and make sure that cattle weren't exposed to it in abundance. "Are you thinking this could be the problem? It is a good bit, but the cattle are getting plenty of other food sources. It should balance out."

Excitement shown in Gabi's eyes. "Unless—" She reached into her backpack and drew out her book. She flipped through and stopped on the page about Careless Weed, scanning it. "Yes! I thought so. If the soil level has a high content of nitrogen, it can make the plant *highly* lethal. It can change the plant from a low, managed risk to deadly. Sudden death can occur with no previous signs. And that's what we think is happening to your cattle. I have a good feeling about this, Jess. The lab work will prove it when it comes back. God is good. This is the best-case scenario. All you have to do now is mow down this stuff."

Jess grinned like a kid watching the pleasure on Gabi's face. "I think you could be on to something," he said, excitement mixed with hope and relief hummed through him. Like she'd said, if this was the culprit, this was manageable and containable.

She laughed, popped to her feet like a jack-in-the-box and held out her hand for a high-five. "I smell success! And I *like* the way it smells."

Looking at her, Jess chalked it up to the excitement and opened his big mouth. "I like the way you look, too," he blurted out, grinning like a fool. There was so much to like about Gabi.

Except for that drinking problem.

"Jess, I need to tell you something," Gabi said, standing among the Careless Weeds. She was so happy to find what she was fairly positive was Jess's problem. But she'd realized that she couldn't put off the inevitable any longer. She had to come clean.

When Phillip walked out on her there had been none of this, no heartache that reached inside her and threatened to break her in two as he walked out the door. With Jess, he'd just walked inside the door of her heart and she was frightened beyond anything she'd ever known that, when she was completely transparent about herself, he'd walk right out and never look back.

Despite that risk, it was time.

"When I told you about myself, about my problem, I didn't tell you everything. And knowing how you feel about certain things, I know that I have to be totally open with you."

His eyebrows dipped in consternation. "I thought you had been."

Her stomach twisted. "Not about everything."

He gave her an encouraging smile that made her sadder than she could stand. Oh, how she loved this man.

"When I became a Christian I changed a lot. God turned my life around. I told you I got behind the wheel that night but Jess, I…I drank a lot. Me driving while intoxicated was not just a first-time occurrence on that night that I almost killed those kids." She saw the surprise flash in his eyes. Felt him stiffen though he was standing two feet away. But she pressed on.

"The truth is I drank almost every day, and I drank a lot. I lived for the weekend when I could drink as much as I wanted and party till I dropped and didn't have to worry about showing up at work without a hangover."

She closed her eyes against the churning storm she saw brewing in Jess's eyes. "I'm not proud of this, but I can't begin to tell you how many times I woke up and couldn't remember where I was." Embarrassment washed over her but she continued. "Or how I got there."

Jess's eyes had darkened with anger. His lips were flattened, grim. She prayed when she was done it would make a difference…and yet something inside her was dimming. Hope was fading with each word.

"I was out of control, Jess, I—I'd gotten to where I needed alcohol every day. I wanted it."

He made a harsh sound and glared down at the hard ground. "I should have known—" The words were bitter and cut right to Gabi's heart.

She blinked away the dampness in her eyes; she would not tear up. "When Judy told me in no uncertain terms what I had almost done that night, and then told me about her son, I broke. God laid His hand on me and all Gram and my mother's prayers came together and I saw what I was going to become—*had* become. I knew it would only get worse if I didn't turn around and run to God's loving arms. Jess, I knew that I loved alcohol too much and that soon, I wouldn't be able to turn away from it at all. I have a problem, but I can tell you with complete honesty and with all my heart that God opened my eyes in time. I walked away and I don't have a problem any longer. *I don't.* I don't drink any more. I don't *have* to have it. I don't have a problem any longer."

"Why are you just now telling me this? You could have told me before."

"You're right." Her heart squeezed tight with fear. "I didn't tell you because, in my heart of hearts I didn't want you to think badly of me."

She waited, wanting to feel his arms around her.

"You should have told me," he said, then turned and walked through the trees. Gabi followed.

"Jess, I lov—" she bit the words back "—I'm not that person anymore."

He swung around. "Do you *know* how many times I heard my dad tell my mother he'd quit? That he wasn't that person any more?" He laughed harshly, his eyes glittering in the dappled light. "Until one day he told her 'this is who I am—deal with it'."

Gabi fought back tears, her hands shook and she hugged herself against the pain in his words.

"Gabi, I told you, *you knew,* I will never have that happen in my life. You lied to me when you chose not to tell me who you are."

Despite all the pain and guilt she was already feeling, this stunned her. *You lied to me when you chose not to tell me who you are.* She couldn't move, watching him disappear through the trees.

He was right.

She had lied to him about who she was. She had lied to him by holding back the most important detail of her life.

And now it had come between them.

Chapter Nineteen

Jess drove straight to the hill overlooking the lake. It hit him the minute he pulled up that he'd started to envision him and Gabi building a home here and having kids grow up on this beautiful spot.

The thought sent a dagger through his heart. How had this all happened so quickly? A fierce longing shot through him, perspiration beaded across his forehead—he loved Gabi Newberry.

He closed his eyes and slammed the walls around his heart tightly closed. He'd never brought any other woman to this spot and yet he'd brought Gabi here—his heart had known before he'd acknowledged it.

Slamming his hand against the steering wheel, he welcomed the pain to that of his heart cracking wide open.

Getting out of the truck he stalked to the edge of the hill and glared at the lake below.

How could I have been so stupid?

He'd known in his gut from the very beginning that she had a problem. She'd almost killed a carload of kids, for cryin' out loud. How could he have let that just slide by?

He raked his hands through his hair, realized he'd taken his hat off, chucking it to the seat as he'd driven across the pastures. She'd lied to him and let him fall in love with her.

But he'd known.

He had no one to blame but himself.

When you knew someone had a problem you didn't want to deal with, the rule of thumb was you got out immediately. You took no risk of letting the unthinkable happen, no risk of opening up your heart and then having it shredded.

Jess knew he had no one to blame but himself.

Gabi called in sick to work the next two days, after what had happened between her and Jess. She'd stayed awake all night crying and berating herself for not having been honest with Jess in the first place. She'd searched her Bible for peace and God had given her a message of love over and over again. Still, her heart was crushed and she longed for Jess.

His father had lied to him, over and over again—the man who should have been his hero, let him down, time and time again. And then his mother had abandoned him and his brothers. Just left them there with a man who cared more for his drink than his family. She hurt for Jess and yet, she'd wanted so much to be the one God would place in his life to give him the kind of love and support he'd never known.

Gabi cried, hurting for him as much as for herself. How had this happened?

Her Gram called, but Gabi didn't pick up the phone. She knew Adela would pick up on her sadness and the fact that something was wrong but she just couldn't talk about it. Not even to her beloved grandmother.

By one o'clock Gabi was numb. When someone knocked on her door, Gabi's heart raced with hope that maybe Jess had come.

"Gabi, honey, are you all right?" Adela's sweet voice rang through the house as Gabi heard the door open. Of course her Gram had a key.

Before she could scramble out of bed Adela Ledbetter Green was standing in the bedroom staring at her with tender eyes. "Honey, what in the world has happened?"

Adela rushed to sit on the bed next to Gabi. Her hand on Gabi's arm was all it took. Gabi proceeded to spill her guts to her grandmother in between tears. "This was all my fault," she cried, after she'd gotten most of the truth out, including her confession to her Gram about her drinking problem.

"Of course Jess would be skeptical. His father probably told him all the time that he was going to quit drinking," she continued, tears spilling out of the edges of her eyes.

"Gabi, look at me," Adela said, her sweet voice firm and gentle at the same time. Gabi looked at her.

Adela smiled. "The difference is you *did* quit."

Gabi shook her head. "But there's always the chance I could fall off the wagon. I'm an alcoholic. End of story."

"Gabi, I'm not saying you don't have a problem and I'm not saying your road will always be easy. But how have you done during this crisis? Have you wanted to find a bottle?"

Gabi dabbed at her eyes. "No. Actually, I haven't." Relief washed over Gabi.

"Have you prayed about all of this?"

Gabi nodded, feeling stronger by the second.

"Then I'd say you're doing all right. Maybe you can talk to Brady and Dottie out at the No Place Like Home women's shelter and see what kind of advice they might be able to give you."

Gabi nodded, feeling better but still heartsick.

"Let's get you out of that bed, honey. You are

one strong cookie and with God at your side, you can do all things. Face all trials and find joy in the morning. Remember, you've committed your life to God and it is a two-way street. Now He is committed to you and He promises that He will never leave you or forsake you. And neither will I."

Tears welled in her heart and flowed to her eyes, looking at the vivid blue glow of her Gram's eyes. God was there for her. No matter what happened in her life today, tomorrow or all the days of her life. With her Gram and God on her side, she could survive anything.

"What's going on, Jess?"

Jess shot Luke a glare. "Nothing." He'd called Luke and told him about the Careless Weed, and that it needed to be mowed down. Then he'd hit the road for three days. Only coming back because he knew Luke needed help with the Mule Hollow rodeo.

Luke huffed an impatient laugh. "Don't give me that, Jess. You're talking to me. And you're about to break those steel gates in half you're slamming them so hard." Moving to stand directly in front of him, Luke rammed a fist to his hips. "I'm not going anywhere until you talk to me."

"Leave it be, Luke."

"Not this time, brother. What's happened? It doesn't take a genius to figure out something must have happened between you and Gabi. What's up?"

Jess scowled and said nothing.

"Being irresponsible has never been your motive. I heard something was wrong with Gabi, too. She didn't go to work for two days. She also isn't talking, according to what I hear up at Sam's. And yes, in case you're interested, the soil tested off the charts in nitrogen levels making those Careless Weeds extremely toxic."

"Did you get it all mowed down?" Jess asked, guilt eroding his temper.

"Yeah, I did. Now fess up, Jess, what happened?"

"She *lied* to me, Luke. Gabi has a real problem with drinking. She came clean out there in the meadow." He stared at his brother, hating that a world of pain was probably shinning in his eyes. "After I fell in love with her. She told me that she might have a problem." He raked his hands through the hair at the back of his hat.

"You love her." Hope vibrated in Luke's words.

"Did you not hear me? She used to drink so much she'd black out." The thought disgusted him. And imagining Gabi like that was so far removed from anything he'd ever envisioned of her that his stomach sickened thinking about it. A messed-up drunk was not a pretty sight. He'd seen it plenty with his dad.

"But she told you she doesn't do that anymore."

"That's what she said."

"So you don't believe her?"

Jess braced one hand on the trailer and dug the toe of his boot into the dirt. "I don't believe she doesn't have a problem anymore."

"Ahh," Luke said. "I see. Like Dad."

Jess didn't say anything. The last thing he'd ever wanted to do was compare Gabi to his father. But that was the measuring stick he had.

"Jess, you know I love you. But you're messing up here."

"You don't think this is tough for me? You think I wanted this?"

"No. But you're taking the easy way out and I don't like it. We've never had it easy. I don't know why that is, but that's just the way the bull bucks. We take what life gives us and we learn to deal with it. We learn to move with the spin and we ride for the full eight seconds. We don't jump off early and we good-and-well don't stay face-down in the dirt. That's not the way we roll. God didn't make us that way."

Jess was going to say something but Luke cut

him off. "I'm not finished. So what if we were given one of the tougher bulls to ride—we are better men because of it. Don't you see that? You are always going to be alone if you don't take some kind of risk."

"Luke, just because I'm choosing not to risk a repeat of our childhood for myself or my future kids, *if* I decide someday to take that risk, doesn't mean you can sit back and judge me. Back off, bro. There is responsibility there and it sits on *my* shoulders, not yours. Do you get that? This is my life we're talking about."

Luke surprised Jess by laughing harshly. "Man," he said. "You got it right when you say you can choose. Life is about choices. God gives us free will to make choices. You're right, you *are* responsible not only for your choices affecting your future but how you let your past affect your future." He shook his head and looked disappointed in Jess. It cut deeper than Jess wanted it to. This was the worst disagreement they'd ever had and it caught Jess by surprise.

Luke continued, his eyes full of concern. "I was hoping you'd decide that life isn't without risk. If there was one thing our background taught you, I thought for certain it was that if you love someone, sometimes you have to fight for them, not abandon them when times are rough, or details aren't exactly how you wanted them to be. Don't you get it? You *love* her, Jess."

Jess stared at his brother. Luke didn't often lose his cool but he was angry. They stared hard at each other, cattle kicked and bellowed and time ticked on.

"You need to think about it. How willing are you to see her walking down the streets of Mule Hollow every day and know you walked away? You better think about this—better yet, maybe it's time you got down on your knees and did a little praying. It's been too long, this grudge you've got with God. You don't think God's ever done anything worthwhile in your life—He very well could have just offered you a treasure and you tossed it away without even blinking an eye." Luke wagged his head in disgust and strode off. At the exit of the arena, he turned around.

"It's ironic that you're working so hard not to repeat your past, and yet in a way, you're repeating it. You're walking away just like Mom did." Luke gave an exasperated grunt. "We needed her and she walked away because she couldn't handle it. Gabi needs you and you're not even stepping up to the plate because you can't handle it."

Shaking his head in disgust, Luke strode

toward his truck, his spurs clinked with each step, the sound was a jab to Jess's heart.

Luke's disappointment in him stung. When Jess got in his truck, he grabbed the wheel and laid his head on his gloved hands. "Lord..." The word slipped from his lips, in the hot, silent cab. Jess's throat ached and his heart burned. He tried to add, *help me*. But the words didn't come.

Chapter Twenty

The second Mule Hollow Homecoming Rodeo went off with flying colors. Gabi went because Gram wanted her there. The place was packed. As Gabi crossed the parking lot the sound of Norma Sue's husband, Roy Don, could be heard on the PA system welcoming all the Mule Hollow people who were there.

Gabi was doing well, thinking positive. Putting one foot in front of the other. And she was determined to hold her head high should she run into Jess. And to be friends.

She hoped she didn't run into him.

She hoped she *did* run into him.

Susan knew what was going on. She'd figured it all out when Gabi had suddenly gotten ill. Gabi hadn't had the heart to deny it. Especially since Susan had been the first one to point out that Gabi cared for Jess. Nope, Gabi *loved* Jess.

Susan had also given her firm orders before she left work that day. "If you run into Jess, smile and show him what he's missing. Do not show him he's hurt you. He'll figure things out and he'll come running. Some guys are just a little dense where love is concerned."

Gabi knew their problem was deeper than Susan realized, but that was exactly what her plan was. Smile. And keep on walking.

Several people called to her as she entered the arena and walked toward the stands. She relaxed with each person she spoke to. It was so nice to live in a town where folks knew her and welcomed her.

She was almost to the stands and could see all three of the Mule Hollow matchmaking posse sitting on the fifth row up. Her eyes were on them when she heard that familiar voice beside her.

"Hi, Gabi."

She turned to find Jess standing inside the arena beside the entrance gate. Bars were between them.

"Jess," she said, no smile on her face, but her voice was strong. Peppy. "Looks like it's going to be a good night," she said, as if she were talking to a stranger.

"Yeah, good crowd." He looked a bit stunned.

Gabi wondered if she looked the same. Maybe not, but she was determined she wasn't going to sound it. She smiled, despite the nerves churning in her stomach. He had warned her that he wouldn't love an alcoholic.

Gabi smiled bigger, feeling her dimple crease her cheek with sincerity. Yes, he had warned her. She'd fallen in love with him with open eyes. "You have a good night, Jesse James," she teased, her throat thickening with the threat of tears. "It's all okay."

Sunday morning came and the inkling of hope in the back of her mind that Jess might have come by to talk to her after the rodeo last night faded. She'd been disappointed and come to church knowing she was probably going to get the third degree from Esther Mae and Norma Sue. They'd badgered her all night at the rodeo as they'd been doing all week. Gabi tried to keep things private but like Susan, they'd assumed far too much that was accurate.

Still, she needed to come to church, needed to move forward. Adela had told her to hang on because God had a plan.

Adela had also reminded her that God had made Gabi spunky and outspoken for a reason and not to forget that. And it was that personality that Jess had fallen in love with. Adela's prayer was that Gabi's love and strength would help heal his heart and mend the wounds from his past. That would take time and patience. Gabi was fighting to have patience, because try as she might, she was still struggling on that end.

She was sitting in the pew beside Adela and Sam when halfway through the message the church door creaked opened. She didn't look over her shoulder to see who the latecomer was but Esther Mae did. Her yellow and purple-grape-encrusted hat rotated as she turned to peek from two rows in front of Gabi. A huge smile burst across her face and her gaze shot to Gabi. Gabi refused to turn but her heart stuttered, wondering if it could be—

"Mind if I sit here?" Jess whispered, grasping the edge of the pew with his hand and bending near her ear.

Gabi's pulse skittered. Sam and Adela scooted down immediately. Gabi had no other option but to follow them. A mudslide of emotions converged upon her as he squeezed in beside her.

What was he doing here in church, sitting beside her as if nothing had happened?

As if he hadn't broken her heart!

She was tearing up—oh, no, she could not

cry. The very idea of crying in front of him was worse than the whole town thinking she'd needed to be rescued every day by the big buffoon!

Needless to say she did not hear any more of the sermon. Instead, she looked straight ahead, willed her pulse to slow down and fought the urge to elbow the man right in the ribs.

Maybe if she jabbed him hard enough, it might jolt him to open that stubborn heart of his and see that he was losing out on not only her love, but God's love.

Thankfully she made it through the service without using her elbow as a weapon, but she was steaming by the time it was over. Sitting beside him and feeling his eyes—and that of the entire congregation—on her did not lend itself to the best of moods. The instant Chance finished his prayer, Gabi made her move. Squeezing between a startled Adela and Sam, she moved along with the rest of the folks exiting the pew. She refused to stand in front of all of Mule Hollow and make small talk. She just wasn't going to do it. She'd thought she could manage it last night at the arena but couldn't.

The side exit wasn't too many steps from the end of her pew and there were just a few people blocking her way. Escape was possible.

"Gabi, wait," Jess called, right behind her.

She didn't look back at him. Four steps and she would be out the door.

"Gabi, stop. Please."

The soft pleading in his voice and the warm touch of his hand on her arm had her looking over her shoulder at him. He was right there behind her. The man looked so handsome, his longish hair curling beneath his ears, his blue eyes imploring her to stop.

A groan rumbled through her. "Jess, this is not the place for this."

"Why?" he asked, soft but loud enough for anyone paying attention to catch. "I think it's perfect."

She rounded on him. "Don't you see all these people?" she hissed under her breath. The side exit was at the front of the church. She glanced around and just as she'd feared, everyone was watching them.

"You're making a scene, Jess."

"We need to talk."

"I'm warning you that if I start talking, you are not going to want all these witnesses."

That grin she loved rolled across his face with the ease of a man who did not know what was about to hit him!

"Give me your best shot, sweetheart."

"Go ahead, Gabi," Norma Sue called from two rows in front of her. "Get it out in the open."

"That's right, go for it." Esther Mae giggled, making her grapes do a little jig on top of her head.

Jess grabbed Gabi's hand, finally realizing privacy would be the smart move. He led her across the choir loft and into the tiny choir room. The room was dark and small. And crowded with chairs. It felt much like the closet they'd been in the day of the cobbler contest.

The door was barely closed behind them when Jess stepped up and took her face between his hands.

"I'm sorry, Gabi."

His words were tender. His eyes were the same. And her heart was hanging in the balance as she fought not to fall to pieces at his words.

"Y-you should be," she managed to say.

"I know you want to knock me in the head for my behavior."

He didn't have a clue.

His hands felt so lovely though, cupping her face, and he was mere inches from her as he spoke. But she pulled away, needing to put some distance between them.

"Jess," she said, finding herself again. "I'm no good for you. You will never be able to feel secure with a person like me."

"I'm in love with a person like you. And I'm

secure knowing she loves me, too. Or at least she did. Does she still?"

His eyes were so teal she wanted to dive into them. Her heart was thundering at the look in them. "What does that mean?"

"It means, I love you, Gabi. And I've been a first-rate fool."

"No, Jess, you haven't been. You are a man who used to be a boy and you were hurt very badly."

"I was a boy who thought God didn't care about everyone. But I know different now, because of you."

Gabi couldn't speak.

"You changed me, Gabi. I've been talking with my mother and we're working on mending fences. That's because of you."

"I'm so glad."

His gaze never wavered from hers. "I'm promising you I will never think that again. And I'm asking you to forgive me just like I asked God to forgive me."

Her breath was labored and her head was pounding.

"Jess, I can forgive you, but, I don't know if I can—" She wanted to throw herself into his arms. But he was only apologizing. And she needed some dignity here.

"Jess, no—" He pulled her into his arms and she couldn't move.

"Gabi, I was a fool. I lived my life being afraid of my past and angry at God. You told me once that He'd protected me and you were right. He did, but I didn't want to see that because I was hanging on to my anger so fiercely. Luke pointed out that God was there with me through everything. And He was. My parents weren't, but God was. And until recently when Luke got hold of me, until you came along, I couldn't see how He was always giving me what I needed. What I need now is you, Gabi. And I was so caught up in the past, I hate that I almost passed up on the treasure God has sent into my life."

Gabi's knees were weak.

"I love you, Gabi. The path of my life was worth it if that's what it took to lead me to you."

"Oh, Jess! I love you, too. But…the alcohol. I understand. And you warned me enough."

"Gabi, I'm here for you. I want to be the man my dad wasn't. I want to stand up for the ones I love, you and our children."

Could this be happening? "No, Jess. I can't let you say this. You need to know and be totally sure where my past is concerned. I get where you were coming from. I understand. And I can tell you with confidence that I'm okay but I've signed up to attend AA meetings at the shelter once a month and to be assigned a sponsor. I don't want to take any chances."

Jess went still. "You'd do that, for me?"

She nodded. "For us. But I can tell you that I don't want it any more. When you walked away from me, it broke my heart but it showed me how far I've come with God's help. I didn't need or want to turn to a bottle, Jess. I turned to God."

Jess's eyes misted in that moment and he closed them momentarily before looking earnestly at her. "Gabi, it doesn't matter. I'm here for you either way. I want to stand by you always. I want to love and cherish you. If you'll have me."

His words touched her. "I love you, Jess, but I need you to know and believe that I'm not that person that I used to be. God saved me, and I'm a new person. Do you believe that?"

He smiled. "I believe you."

She heard the certainty in his voice and her heart soared. "Oh, Jess, and to think I was ready to elbow you a few minutes ago."

He chuckled, his beautiful eyes crinkling merrily. "I would have deserved it."

She shook her head. He hiked a brow and she grinned. "Okay, maybe a little you deserved it."

He laughed, then kissed her with a passion that stole her breath and befuddled her brain.

"Gabi, I rescued you that first day when you were swimming in the ditch. And now, you are rescuing me and pulling me up and out of the quicksand I was sinking in. God sent you to me, Gabi, and I almost missed it."

His smile faded and his expression turned serious, his eyes burned with certainty. "After God sent His Son to save my soul, He sent you to renew it with your love."

She closed her eyes and thanked God for all her blessings. "I love you so much, Jess."

He went down on his knees. "Then, will you marry me, and make a family with me?"

Her heart had never felt so full. "Are you sure?"

Jess swept her into his arms and kissed her. "I'm going to live the rest of my life showing you how sure I am. And I'm going to love every minute of it."

"Then I guess we better open this door and tell everyone the good news."

A mischievous grin lit across Jess's face as he pulled her closer. "They can wait," he murmured, and then kissed her with no regrets, full of soaring hope and a promise of more to come…and Gabi decided that Jess had been right all along.

He *had* rescued her that day when he had pulled her out of that raging water and threw her over his shoulder like a sack of potatoes. Who would have ever believed it?

Certainly not Gabi. But boy, was she glad.

Oh, yeah, life was good.

God had a plan and Gabi couldn't wait to see where the rest of that plan took her!

* * * * *

*Be sure to watch for Colt's story,
HER HOMECOMING COWBOY,
coming August 2012
from Love Inspired Books.*

Dear Reader,

Hello and thank you! Thank you all so much for the wonderful support you have shown me and my wacky little town by faithfully reading my Mule Hollow series. This is my twenty-first book, and the twentieth set in Mule Hollow—I cannot believe it! I've so enjoyed the ride and am always thinking of you, my readers, as I create my next stories and try to entertain you with fun while also giving food for thought on how God's goodness can intertwine with and enrich our lives. I hope you are enjoying meeting the Holden men in these three Mule Hollow Homecoming books. Look for Colt's story, *Her Homecoming Cowboy,* coming August 2012. When Colt thinks all is lost…he's about to meet Annie and little Leo, and his life will never be the same!

Do you have someone in your life struggling with addiction? Are you struggling with addiction? Can you see how it is affecting your family? I would love to pray for you or your loved one if you send me a note— Debra Clopton, P.O. Box 1125, Madisonville, Texas 77864, or write to me from my website, debraclopton.com

Until next time, live, laugh and most important, seek God with all your heart.

Debra Clopton

P.S. Remember all the Mule Hollow books are also now ebooks, too. Check my website, www.debraclopton.com, for new things to come!

Questions for Discussion

1. I hope you enjoyed this Mule Hollow story! I had fun writing it, while also touching on deep issues that faced both Gabi and Jess. Throughout the book Gabi is struggling to do and react the way God would want her to react. She is praying for patience and the ability to make good choices. Why is this?

2. Jess doesn't believe he's cut out for love. Why? What is he afraid of?

3. Gabi has a past and is struggling to find her way as a new Christian. What is she seeking when she comes to Mule Hollow?

4. Trying to be true to her need to tell others about Christ and what He's done for her, Gabi boldly asks Jess about his faith when they first meet. How does this make Jess feel?

5. Gabi has a past full of partying and drinking. When she attends the Bible study with many Mule Hollow friends, she decides that no one needs to know about her past. Why does she decide to keep it a secret? How do you feel about her decision?

6. Jess is feeling as if God abandoned him just as his parents did. So he has a lot of resentment inside him. Though he has vowed that his past won't affect his present and is an upbeat guy, we see that his past affects him very much. Do you have this problem in your life, or do you know someone like this? How can you move forward from it or help someone you know to do the same?

7. Jess reveals to Gabi that he feels as if God has something against him and his brothers, and he is confused and angry. Have you ever felt this way?

8. Gabi has come to Mule Hollow looking to be used by God, but in Jess's darkest hour, when she realizes how deep his pain runs, she feels inadequate. Have you ever felt as if you couldn't do what God put before you to do?

9. Do you feel that when you are struggling with feelings of inadequacy, that is when you have to trust God more and realize that you can do all things through Him who strengthens you—and not all things through you who strengthens you? In these

times, it's easy then to give the glory to God and not to yourself.

10. In Jess's darkest hour, after Colt's tragic accident, Jess's true feelings about God come out. It's all about what God hasn't done for him. What does Gabi tell Jess?

11. Gabi counts herself as Jess's friend. A good friend will tell you when you are wrong, even if it is a hard truth and goes against what you want to hear. Gabi does this when she tells Jess he needs to get on his knees and ask God to forgive him. Have you ever had a friend who was wrong about something and you pointed this out to him or her? What was the consequence of being truthful? (Sometimes it is not received well and sometimes it is.) Please discuss ways to help these situations.

12. Jess resents his mother deeply, but when she finally asks him for forgiveness, he realizes that as a child he did not get to make the decision about how his life would go. But now he does have control over making that choice. What does he choose to do and how does he view it?

13. Luke is the most influential person in Jess's life. If he hadn't taken on the responsibili-

ties and made the choices that he made for his own life, how do you believe this would have affected Jess's life? Do you know people whose view on life can ultimately be influenced by your choices for good or bad? Do you seek God's will as Luke did to make the choices that go with how the Bible would lead you?

14. Gabi had wonderful people in her life— her mother and her Gram—and yet she still chose the wrong path. Though our past can affect our future, it is ultimately our responsibility as to which path to follow. While Gabi was on the wrong path, what were her mother and Adela doing? Are you a prayer warrior for those you love?

15. Gabi's biggest regret when she looks back on her partying past is that she wasn't seeking God's will in her life. Are you seeking God's will in your life?

16. Jess holds his mother's actions against her and yet, as Luke points out to him, he chooses to do a similar thing when he walks away from Gabi—the woman he loves. Do you think the advice and sentiments Luke expresses in that confronta-

tion ring true? And again, Luke could have said exactly what Jess wants to hear, but he chooses to say the truth, even though it's not what Jess wants to hear. Instead Luke chooses to say what Jess needs to hear. Do you agree?

17. Montana and Gabi discuss how wonderful life is when your life and God's will collide in unity. God has plans for each of us. How can you feel His will in your life more clearly? Seek it? More Bible time? Please discuss with your reading group how you can be a support for each other.

Love Inspired®
SUSPENSE
RIVETING INSPIRATIONAL ROMANCE

Watch for our series of edge-
of-your-seat suspense novels.
These contemporary tales
of intrigue and romance
feature Christian characters
facing challenges to their faith...
and their lives!

AVAILABLE IN REGULAR
& LARGER-PRINT FORMATS

For exciting stories that reflect traditional values,
visit:
www.ReaderService.com